An Opportune Proposal

Butterton Brides
Book 3

Copyright © 2024 by Ann Elizabeth Fryer

All rights reserved.

No portion of this book may be reproduced in any form without written permission from the publisher or author, except as permitted by U.S. copyright law.

This is a work of fiction. Similarities to real people or events are entirely coincidental.

For my husband, Mark Fryer,
who is always my hero.

Chapter One

December 22, 1810

Chilham, England

I shivered in the empty rooms of the manse. Our belongings had to be sold after Father's passing, there'd been no other choice. I hadn't a farthing to my name. Unless that is, the inheritance Father had always expected came directly to me and no one else.

Alas, the court's propensity to meddle within distant family dramas betwixt long-deceased cousins may cause my potential affluence to go in another direction entirely. Such is the fate of most women as men inherit much of what is left to be inherited. The firstborn male of any family to be exact. Only in my case, another distant female is thick in the game of tangled family lines. Not a man, of course, or this would have certainly been settled months ago. I am sure of it.

I ran my hand across the deep window sill where I used to sit when I was very small while Father scribbled away at sermons. Here, I'd engraved my own name with a pen knife in tiny letters near the right-hand corner: Jane Hartford. It yet remains.

As do I.

I can still see Father's dark head of hair bent over large tomes, with his ready smile and patient answers to my childish questions about life. I closed my eyes and felt his arms gather me up from my perch to the kitchen for gingerbread. How I missed him. There is nothing—no nothing—like a good father's embrace.

Another would take his place here. Would that man's children sit where I had?

I moved away from the dear window seat. I needed to gather my wits—let go of what once was and face the facts gathering like debts at my door. Life moved on and so must I. It had been two years since his passing and settling my plans was long overdue.

The Church had been more than generous in allowing me to stay in the home of my youth as the local curate had been a single gentleman whose cottage was sufficient for the time. But no longer. His position had risen beyond curate, he'd married, and a second child would arrive this month. My house was very much required.

I didn't mind. Not really. The church had a right to take it back. Indeed, the bishop had been too kind in his letter to me a few weeks prior. *I pray the Lord to send a godly gentleman for you to marry*, he'd said, *as soon as may be. So that your future may be secure.*

He'd been so insistent. And hopeful.

A certain security may be found in such a match, to be sure. And yet—I have seen where women have married men for that singular design: security. And while food may be on the plate, the spirit is empty. Her cup doesn't overflow and a grimness wraps her mouth where a smile had once been.

But the good bishop said to pray for a "godly gentleman." He would be surprised to hear my list of what constitutes one. I giggled. Such a man would have children running about him. He'd have a kind word for the lonely. He wouldn't be afraid to muddy his breeches to do a good deed.

He wouldn't flash coin or smile to impress like Arthur Melling had. His very name left a bad taste in my mouth. To think I'd once thought he desired to court me only to find his behavior the same with other girls in the village. Such insincerity. I must toss the memory, it did me no service to think of him.

"Come, Jane, you daydream again. Shut the door so the new mistress doesn't catch cold." Mrs. Jones' bonnet feather shuddered in the chill breeze.

I closed the door, my hand lingering on the shiny brass handle as I hesitated on the front step. Mrs. Jones snatched my hand into her gloved one and led me down. She carried a bundle of bright holly I'd picked for our Christmas celebration in but a few days. Green pointed tips, bright berries, guarded beauty...

"Come now, dear. Best you say goodbye to the manse quickly and be done with it, I say. God's work doesn't tarry. And neither should you."

Her little sermon made me laugh. For Mrs. Jones is the one who taught me that being still before the Lord was a work in itself. His work. The kind that put myself out of the way and God in the center of it.

"My whole life has been lived in that house, Mrs. Jones." I paused and turned again to look up to the window of the room that had been my refuge only last night.

"Mmm." She looped her arm in mine. "Time to dream in other places." Her black peppered curls poked from beneath her bonnet, her smile still youthful. "And at this moment, I'm dreaming of a hot cup of tea before the fire—and some of Angel's biscuits."

I agreed. "Especially Angel's biscuits." How I would miss them.

Mrs. Jones' generosity towards me had been unwavering. I'd often wished she could have been my mama as my own had died when I was small. She'd stepped in as often as she could to offer love and wisdom. Sir Jones, too, when he wasn't busy with his handful of tenants.

We stepped through the gates of Glen Park, such as it was. A little muddy, much trampled, and the brick house of definite vintage. The left parapet had been missing a section for many years, giving it a rather gaping toothless appearance. Songbirds liked to nest there in the spring, crows huddled there now.

Land had been sold off long ago, and the tenants were clustered within sight of this tall and narrow house on the edge of the village. I'd always felt welcome.

Sir Jones anticipated his manservant to the door and flung it open himself. "My dears! Come in and set you down." His bright red cheeks and wide smile bespoke an ever-present cheer. Rare was the occasion that he frowned. Once, when a child had been wounded, and the other when my father died.

"Capital, capital." He placed an arm around me. "Just when you think life is bleak…" he snapped his fingers, "A miracle flickers to life."

"Dear husband." Mrs. Jones set aside her cloak. "Do not be mysterious. Out with it." She winked at me.

He pulled letters from his pocket. "One unopened missive for you, Jane. And one written directly to us, wifey." His grin broadened.

I took the sealed parchment from his hands. From Butterton? Isn't that where my distant cousin lived? The one who might succeed the tiny fortune in limbo? Why on earth did Sir Jones call it a miracle?

"Come, let us allow her to read such news in privacy." He clapped his hands together and looked to Mrs. Jones, as though recalling an important detail. "Cook made the Blum's wedding cake this morning and she is quite angry with me."

She shook her head. "You didn't."

His wide, pleasant face feigned innocence. "Twas only a small piece, my dear. I don't see why it matters so very much. It is meant to be eaten, is it not?"

"I would have had your head, husband."

"Then it's a good thing you aren't the cook, wifey. But do put her at ease for my sake?"

I laughed at their retreating backs. Staying here, even briefly, would be a daily entertainment.

I opened the letter to read what news my titled stranger-cousin would deign to send me…

Dear Miss Hartford,

May I call you dear cousin instead? You may not remember, but we have indeed met—once upon a time. You were newly arrived and when your mother introduced us, you gripped my finger and didn't let go for the passing of thirty seconds. Lord Camden and I had begged your parents for a room for the night as our coach needed repair. Without their kindness, I don't know what we would have done as we were on the way back to Butterton with all haste.

It has come to our attention through our solicitor, Mr. Stevens, Esq., that you are quite alone and have been recently turned out of your father's vicarage. My dear. You must know that you can depend upon good family, no matter what situation lies in our pasts—that neither of us has control over. You must come abide with us. Stay at Butterton Hall where we can look after you and introduce you to such polite society as we are acquainted with. Besides that, I desire to know the infant grown woman and see if she is anything like her beloved mother. I certainly hope so.

We will wait out the courts together. Either way, you shall be cared for. I make this promise. Lord Camden is in full agreement with this plan. I implore you. Do say yes.

At the New Year, I will send a coach to collect you.

Sincerely,

Lady Camden

I didn't know if I liked this abrupt change of plans. Sir Jones seemed elated over the news that my relations desired to oversee my welfare. A miracle, he'd said. Or a mistake? I wondered.

It was one thing to leave the home of my youth—another to leave my village entirely. Each paving stone and every shop, and the families that my father had served were imprinted upon my heart. How could I simply cut myself away from the cloth from which I'd been tightly woven?

Life here was good with much good left to be done. Old friends that I loved. My future rather loomed with a reality I hadn't wanted to see.

The Joneses were so kind to take me in while I prayed and considered my few options: school teacher? Governess? Companion to some elderly gentlewoman?

Oh, I didn't want to leave, but I knew deep down I would have to do so to secure such a position. The bishop desired me to marry—but there was no one here who I could desire to spend the rest of my life with—as if I had a choice in the first place. Which I didn't.

I took a deep breath and looked to the peeling plaster and cracked marble floor. Mud smeared the white squares. Sir Jones had not employed the boot scrape. Again.

The scullery maid appeared with a mop and bucket to wash away his careless mess. I smiled at her before joining my hosts in the parlor. I'd been no stranger to the mop-bucket.

He stood when I entered, brushing biscuit crumbs from his waistcoat. "What say you, gel? Are you not taken aback by the very generosity of your family?"

My family? Were unknown distant cousins to be included in that precious word?

Mrs. Jones patted the seat beside her, poured a cup of tea and added a generous serving of milk. I took it—why had my hands gone trembly? The tea would settle me.

"I am shocked, in all honesty."

Sir Jones filled his pipe, tamping down his tobacco along with the truth of his opinion. "Miracles are shocking, are they not? In the best way."

"But…" I nibbled my bottom lip. "Do you think I should go? I would hate to impose—"

"Oh, but think of the opportunities the Camdens can afford you!" He lowered his voice as if sharing a secret. "You know, we are humble here."

I noted the threadbare carpet, his mended coat… And the fact that Mrs. Jones did indeed help with the housekeeping though she was gentle-born. She, like me, was familiar with occasional chapped hands from washing clothes – and dishes.

And here I was, another mouth to feed when someone else in this village might benefit from the Jones' generosity. At any rate, I'd have to leave here after the holidays—as soon as I found a promising position. Another duty the good bishop promised to help me with if a husband could not be procured.

Sir Jones was right. This seemed a miracle. The Camden's connections would indeed afford a better pool of work options. Father always recounted from the Psalms that the Lord ordered our steps…

I knew when I glanced into Sir Jones' and his dear wife's hopeful faces that I would alight the carriage for Butterton.

My stomach squeezed. This would be my last Christmas in Chilham.

Sir Jones stood and tucked one hand into his vest. "They mean to brisk you about into society! Imagine that, dear girl! You shall do handsomely, I shouldn't wonder."

"Brisk me about in society? Whatever do you mean?"

Mrs. Jones pointed to their letter. "It says here that they plan to sponsor your debut, introduce you to gentleman. See you to a secure future."

Her words buckled that one continuously nagging truth into place. I needed a secure future, for certain. But would it include a young gentleman? Only God knew.

Christmas came with much festive singing, three stuffed geese, one plum pudding, and an overabundance of roasted apples and chestnuts. The Joneses included everyone in the household—the apples made up for slim pickings from the geese. Yet another indication that my journey to Butterton was so very necessary.

At the New Year, then. How fitting that this distinct change in my life should begin then...on the first day of an unknown year...

But the carriage didn't come on the day of my determined departure. Surprisingly, it came three days prior—with a grim-faced stranger to accompany me up the long road to Butterton. The housekeeper, it seemed, had been sent to fetch me in time for the New Year's Eve party, with but a day to spare for my welcome.

Chapter Two

Such a cold and stunningly quiet journey—not that I've journeyed anywhere far from home before. The housekeeper had seemed relieved to have a night of un-jostled rest before embarking on the return trip. But that relief evolved into a complete placidity by the next day. Never had I encountered a more disengaged individual. Never. I did my best to offer a little companionable conversation. Hour by hour, I spoke of the scenery, the weather. And what must Butterton be like?

"Like any other village, I imagine." Her unsmiling square chin shut to further query. I wondered how, if my hostess was so good to send a companion for my journey, that they should send this sour apple—the housekeeper no less. Perhaps none else would suit. Or perhaps she suffered from a pain in her legs and preferred to do so in silence. Her knitting would stay put away. But there, in the corner of her seat was a tiny knit stocking. Must have fallen from the small bag traveling by her side. Had she a grandchild? I hoped she offered the tike many more smiles than me.

A few grunts and nods would be the extent of her personal engagement with me. Without a comforting companion by my side, I was left alone with my thoughts, nerves twisting together into a tight rope around my middle. Perhaps I should have stayed with good Sir Jones, despite my urgent need for employment.

I could not fathom why Lord and Lady Camden wanted a distant poor relation—a vicar's daughter of no consequence—to come live with them. Was there more meaning to this seeming kindness?

No matter the housekeeper's attitude, my hosts did desire my presence and, to my great curiosity, explained that they'd met my mother once upon a time. As they recounted, I had grasped her finger and would not let go. Was this lady's memory a sign from God that I must grasp her hand again?

A few more naps and villages later, in the dark of the early winter's night, we arrived at Butterton Hall.

Before me stood a towering Elizabethan monstrosity of mullioned windows and severe pointed arches. The equally ancient door opened on wide, creaking hinges. I imagined the place appeared much more desirable in the daylight. Truly, this was no cozy Glen Park. I glanced up at a third-story window—a form hovered behind the wavy glass, then moved away. Watching me?

I was ushered swiftly into a small foyer where a clutch of yew and rosemary hung beribboned on the newel post. The housekeeper brushed past, its pungent scent trailing after her. She led me down a winding passage of narrow halls that connected with another landing to the main staircase—a much wider set of stairs like a great swallowing mouth from the shadowed hall.

I was nearly out of breath when the placid woman I'd traveled with gave a sharp word to a much younger maidservant, and then disappeared.

She kindly smiled at our introduction. "They said to give ye the Yellow Room, miss."

I nearly melted at the friendly welcome. The Yellow Room. How nice. I followed her down another turn until she stopped at a door that must be mine. The maid's key rattled in the lock, then pushed the door open. I'd never locked my doors at home. Why was it done so here?

I stepped inside the icy-cold darkness as the maid lit a single candle that highlighted a bed. She lit a few more. Two very small windows positioned near the ceiling—obviously intended to provide light but no pleasure of viewing the outside.

The only things yellow about the room were the crewel work on the bedcovering, and a golden velvet-covered stool—and the candle glow. Altogether charming, yet, I shuddered. Without a good window to see God's wide-open sky and the sunrise, I felt in a cell. I shivered again and thanked God when the maid knelt to light the fire.

"I'll send tea up, miss, and the lads will be at the door with your trunk in a blink."

"I thank you."

A pot of tea arrived with a directive. "You are to join Lady Camden and Mr. Stevens in the library for supper at seven o'clock."

Supper in the library? How odd. Surely, a place such as this boasted a dining room of grand proportion. Never mind that Father and I found it fulfilling to take our repast with a good stack of poetry by our sides. Scones and jam and Shakespeare... a clog formed in my throat, my eyes moistened.

Leaving the manse had been hard enough, letting go of my daily life with Father had been much harder. He was my home, and he was gone. So, I'd endeavored to take those parts I loved about our life with me wherever I went. But supper wouldn't be a mix of jam-scones and sonnets. Regrettably. This place was too fine to stoop to such simple joys.

I daresay finding a little friend who would join me in a duet on the pennywhistle would be impossible. I laughed. If I became a governess, I hoped my students would be eager to learn simple tunes. And smile a great deal.

My trunk appeared as I was thawing from the cold. I snatched my favorite shawl and stretched my weary limbs. This had been the longest day of my life. I had but a single hour to collect myself and become presentable to my benefactress. Would she be pleased with me?

I put on my best black gown which was at least two years old. I'd had it made to properly grieve for Father. I rewound my hair into its regular twist at the back, washed my face in the ice-cold water basin, and shored up my nerves with a prayer.

I wondered if my cousin would regret the offer to introduce me into society. Did I even want to be? I'd scarcely given it a thought. My life generally revolved around villagers and their needs. Not the ballroom or soirees. She would find me sorely lacking and the whole affair an extreme dudgeon. And then perhaps I might get on with my position as companion or governess somewhere else.

A bell rang. Supper. In the library. I opened my bedroom door and glanced down the hall, lit only by a pair of candle sconces, leaving a bouncing glow upon the wall. Did I turn right or left? Alas, no maid had been sent to guide me in this vast, strange place.

Well. One path would lead somewhere, would it not? I turned to the right and found the main stairway again, this time a sconce had been lit, lending scant light to the shadowed steps.

The butler scurried from a corner shadow. I gasped. His many wrinkles scored his face in a startling pattern.

"My apologies." His smile sent the wrinkles into a tight swirl. "Lady Camden awaits you in the library."

"And the library is?" I glanced around.

"Just there." An ancient finger pointed. He turned and left.

The housekeeper and the butler obviously carried a prejudice against one of lesser rank such as I. Was that why I'd been taken up the servant's stairs and not the main staircase? I wondered what they'd been told about me. They should have been informed that I was a gentleman's daughter despite my poverty.

More candle sconces lit a hall of several doors. Had the butler pointed at the door with the arch, or the rectangular door farther down?

A choice had to be made.

I tried the arched door. Yes, this must be it—no. Indeed not. A man straightened his form from standing over billiards, swiping a dark shock of too-long hair away, revealing a rather handsome face. "I do not require refreshment at this time as I am to dine with Lady Camden this evening."

"Pardon me?"

He annunciated slowly. "I do not require anything. Thank you."

Such embarrassment. He barely looked my way, thought me a mere maid. I curtsied and closed the door behind me. The butler must have pointed to the next one. Dear me.

I entered through the following doorway to see an elegant room. On one side were the bookshelves situated in rows and lining the wall. On the other side of the room, a cozy arrangement of couch and a small dining table had been set for three.

A throat cleared, "Is it you, my cousin? Come, let me see you." The woman who must be Lady Camden rose from a stuffed chair by the window.

Her soft words were a welcome to my heart.

Her much bejeweled neck and fingers glittered. As did her smile. "Ah! The babe all grown." She took my hand and raised it to appraise my form. "You are lovely. Simply lovely. I do not doubt the connections I shall be able to make for you, my dear. No doubt at all."

"I thank you for your hospitality. You are too generous." I curtsied.

"Nonsense. You are family." A crimson turban wound around her high-silver hair, her equally crimson gown of a cut I'd not seen before, an overskirt split down the center as a ladybird's wing. The ruffled fichu beneath her chin moved as she spoke. "My nieces left before Christmas. They have abandoned Butterton Hall for the delights of London—and I have no doubt they will gain husbands by the end of the season. No doubt at all." Her eyes gleamed with pleasure. "I imagine you are famished."

My, my. Husbands and hunger mentioned in a single breath. I supposed older women were forever matchmaking. Perhaps she meant only to be helpful.

A door opened at the side of the room.

"There is Mr. Stevens. Our solicitor."

The man from the billiard room. The family's solicitor? He was here? He crossed the room slowly, confusion rising on his face.

"Come be introduced to my cousin, Mr. Stevens. Thanks to your pertinent influence, she has arrived."

He strode before me and bowed. "My apologies, Miss Hartford. I did not know."

Lady Camden's smile faded a little. "Didn't know what?"

I was going to answer but he spoke first. His London accent, an educated one. "To my shame, I assumed she was a maid sent to wait upon me."

I laughed. "It is of no consequence." Were not we all the same in the sight of God? I did not care about being mistaken for an honest laborer. Not one bit.

Lady Camden waved a hand to the dining table. "There'll be no mistaking you for anything else but a debutante after tomorrow's appointment with the drapers."

A queasy wave crashed in my stomach. I didn't want to be anyone but myself, whether I wore this old black gown, or a new one. My grief remained. I feared I'd never be the prize she intended to offer.

Mr. Stevens bit the side of his lip as he pulled a chair for Lady Camden and me to sit. When he took his seat, he sent me a look of regret. Or was it pity? Did I really appear so decidedly below decent society? One would think that if I were to be mistaken for a maid, I should be wearing an apron and mop cap. Indeed.

I would find the carriage and make my way back to the humble Sir Jones and escape this forthcoming escapade. I laughed at what Father must be thinking if he could look down and see me from Heaven.

"Did I say something humorous?" Lady Camden's eyes blinked.

"Ah, no indeed, my lady. I merely laugh at myself."

She placed her napkin on her lap. "How odd. I never heard of a young girl doing such."

"Have you not?" I followed suit with my napkin. "I find laughter helpful to move forward when life is different than expected." Such was often the case.

She grew silent, but Mr. Stevens smiled at my answer and picked up the conversation. "How was your journey?"

The butler slipped beside my elbow and poured wine into my goblet.

How to describe my trip without speaking words of utter boredom? "We were not accosted by highwaymen, did not have a wheel break, and did not run out of peppermint pastilles." Father's idea had been to repeat three positive things after a long, hard day. Counting blessings, he called it.

Mr. Steven's eyes wrinkled in amusement, his smile revealing a tooth chipped at a rather endearing angle. A rush of warmth rose at that thought. Why? I should not lose my wits at the first handsome man I met since arriving. Ridiculous. One did not regard a gentleman's teeth, chipped or no.

He dipped his head. "Arrived in one piece, none too worse for the wear?"

"I am relieved to be on solid ground." I would sleep soundly tonight—I hoped.

"I'm sure you are."

Lady Camden held a fork of meat aloft. "She was rapturous to come here, weren't you? Sir Jones couldn't have been more agreeable to the plan. Any person such as yourself could not refuse."

One of Sir Jones' favorite words. *Rapturous.* I should have known he would reply with so great an enthusiasm. However, her tone could be taken as more callous than kind.

Mr. Stevens cut into his meat. "You have a worthy estate, my lady." He winked at me as though we shared a private joke. "Daylight will reveal its many charms, Miss Hartford." His eyes glinted with humor—as though we were already friends.

"I am sure to be...enraptured." A good night's rest would calm my quickly beating heart and dim the sparkle in his eyes. I was truly overly tired.

Lady Camden dabbed the corners of her lips with her napkin. "Lord Camden is dining with the Chinworth fellow or he would have been here to greet you."

Mr. Stevens paused. "He dines with Tobias Chinworth?"

"One and the same."

A grim line formed about his mouth.

"Oh, I know you recommended he not do so, but once something is in his mind—none can stop him."

She didn't sound particularly concerned. Who was this Tobias Chinworth? I wondered how he mattered to the family—and why Mr. Stevens should care where his employer dined.

Mr. Stevens took a breath and resumed eating his supper, other than short replies to Lady Camden's simplistic queries.

Pensiveness swathed him like a shroud. I recognized the expression. Saw the same on Father's face when working out a conundrum, often between parishioners. Nothing but a good deal of quiet to help. Only here, in the midst of dinner, seemed untimely. Especially after he'd been so amiable. Deep thought had swallowed up his friendliness, leaving only good manners behind.

At length, he excused himself, leaving us alone. I can easily say that a crumb of his good company was worth more than Lady Camden's refined tone and pretty speeches. I wished his return.

My cousin seemed to be the sort who thought extremely well of herself and her position in society and, by way of her position, believed her own intellect superior. Father might call this self-righteousness. And he would not be wrong. She gave the impression that her rank was equal to having both knowledge and wisdom. And I, being the poorer cousin of no rank, needed her generous patronage. And that by such offerings, I might become wise like her. Or at least less menial and simple.

"I shall open the world to you, my dear. The world that is worth knowing, that is." She pursed her lips in a self-satisfied smile.

Her meaning was clear. "I thank you." How else could I respond?

A tray carrying two cups of chocolate was brought in. I'd only ever heard of the luxurious drink. The first sip surprised. The second, my eyes closed involuntarily. By the third, I was indeed thankful I'd come to this new experience. Chocolate was far more delicious than I dreamt it could be. This part of my new world I could well accept!

Lady Camden smiled. "I insist upon it every evening before bed." She set her half-empty cup on the table. "I am glad you have come."

She rose and I did as well. "Take it with you, my dear. I pray you rest well."

This time, a maid was there to take me back to my room. Up that grand staircase and down the narrow dimly lit hall. As we reached my door, a long, painful shriek startled me. The last sips of chocolate spilled down my dress, the mug cracked to pieces on the floor.

Another shriek sounded.

The maid's eyes widened. She quickly curtsied and ran, dripping with the sweet drink as my pulse began to race. I was both embarrassed and worried. What had happened?

Another maid soon appeared. "Never you mind about the noise, miss." She brushed a towel over me. "I shall tend the fire and you'll be right cozy."

"Is someone hurt?"

"Not that I'm aware of." She turned away from me and busied herself, then left as swiftly as she might.

How strange. Though, I suppose an estate of this size employs quite a few people who might have had an accident. I prayed that whoever it was that shrieked received the help that they needed. I cleaned the unfortunate drips from my gown as best as I could and readied for bed.

After hours of sound sleep beneath thick wool blankets, I heard the shriek again. This time, I couldn't shut my eyes again, no matter how hard I tried.

Hopefully, the morning would bring answers.

Chapter Three

I'd been lazily propped up in bed long enough, blinking in the winter darkness. Time to slip out of the warmth. I wished for my journal that I might begin to record the events of January 1, 1811, only the New Year didn't begin until tomorrow. Mrs. Jones's Christmas present for me, along with a jar of black ink.

"A new beginning ought to be recorded. It will be interesting, won't it dear? To see where you began and where you end up at the year's close." Interesting, indeed. A distant cousin vying for an inheritance. Butterton Hall, cups of chocolate, and the strange shrieking I'd heard. Mayhap I'd begin writing in the journal a day early.

I crept from bed and dressed. Even managed to restore the fire with the few hot coals hiding beneath thick ash before the maid arrived with tea and soft, currant-studded buns for my breakfast. A perfect breakfast.

I wouldn't meet Lady Camden again until luncheon to go over party plans. Setting my scribblings aside, I sank my teeth into the soft roll.

From her glamourous vantage point, I wondered what she would think of a humble Christmas at Glen Park. Or my father's vicarage when we had naught but gingerbread and gallons of tea for our celebration with other poor parishioners. I confess an absolute weakness for gingerbread. I very much doubt I'd be allowed freedom in the kitchen to make some.

I nibbled a last bite of the bun, swallowed tepid tea, and when the sun had fully risen, exited my room to do a bit of exploring before I met with Lady Camden. I donned my cloak and made my way down the hall to the staircase.

I'd not had the chance to really observe the foyer—a minor affair compared to a much larger, more modern location that the butler showed me. Here were the Grecian columns and gleaming marble that I'd expected. Shining and new, not at all like Sir Jones' abode. It led into a receiving room, and a grand ballroom, a new dining room that could hold more than one hundred souls.

I had enough of the inside, though altogether lovely, and exited through a side door into the garden and wandered around the hard frozen grounds—so many rose bushes, barren except thorns, withered leaves, and bright hips where the buds had been. An apothecary might have been able to make use of the hips. Why they had not been harvested? Seemed a waste.

Perhaps Lady Camden decorates the Hall with roses in the summer. I shut my eyes and imagined the bright reds and pinks in full bloom. Mayhap yellow roses, too.

"Miss Hartford." A deep voice startled me.

I opened my eyes to a smiling face. "Mr. Stevens. Good heavens...morning. I mean good morning." I replaced surprise with a smile. "I did not see you there." Of course, I hadn't. My eyes had been shut.

His cheeks and nose were turning red from the cold and I began to shiver. Was he as embarrassed as I to find a woman standing in a frozen rose garden with her eyes closed? Must have thought me daft.

He bowed. "Shall we go inside and warm up? I confess I have a bit of business to discuss with you if you have a moment to spare?" He smiled again, those thought lines that had appeared on his face the night before had disappeared.

"I am free until noon."

"Plenty of time, then." He offered his arm and I slipped my gloved hand in. "No one uses the morning parlor, we may have privacy there. I'll ring for tea."

I couldn't imagine what he needed to discuss.

It wasn't until I held a hot cuppa between my hands that he began. First, he paced, then, he sat across from me, tapping his fingers on his cup.

"I wish I didn't need to tell you, and I hope you will forgive me."

"As we have scarcely been in each other's presence for the space of an hour, I hardly think I have anything to forgive."

"No, wait." He took a breath. "The inheritance that's tangled up in the courts? You should know that we represent the Camdens." He blushed. "That is, my father was retained by the

Camdens. I am here to comb through documents and family history. And assist with Lord Camden's... other issue."

"Is that all?" I laughed. I didn't expect to receive the balance in question. I'd released that desire months ago.

"You aren't offended?"

I shrugged. "Your father is merely doing the job he's been hired to do. Why should I be?"

"Because my father rarely loses. And as a result, you will be affected, Miss Hartford."

Why must the value of my life revolve around this inheritance? "If I recall, it was your advice to Lady Camden that I come here."

"It was. Frankly, Miss Hartford, I couldn't bear the thought of a vicar's daughter being alone and helpless."

This sent me into a laughing fit. "Me, helpless?" I was willing to put my hand to any plow, whatever it might be. "Thought God might strike you dead for ignoring a poor righteous mouse such as I?" Laughter refused to stop. "His eye is on the sparrow, Mr. Stevens. And me too."

"You aren't afraid of losing in court?"

My laughter calmed. "I never had the inheritance in the first place. I do not expect to win. Therefore, how could I lose anything? I do not even have a solicitor to represent me in the case. The situation is at the mercy of the judge, whoever he may be. I will accept his decision with neither angst nor anguish."

"You'd confer it to the Camdens?"

"If, by God's design, I gain the inheritance, I wouldn't refuse it. You are right on the count that I am a poor vicar's daughter and quite alone." I swallowed the last of my warm drink. "I thank you for your kindness in informing me of the continued reality of my situation. Your regard for my condition. Even your influence in my coming here." The results of which remained to be seen.

He licked his lips. "You are an unusual woman, Miss Hartford." He set his cup down. "I do hope you enjoy your stay—and Lady Camden's ministrations. Such as they are." He reached inside his coat pocket and pulled out an envelope. "I have been instructed to give you this."

I opened the paper flap. Pounds. Twenty of them.

"By whom?"

"I am not at liberty to say."

Though I could guess. The Camdens also felt guilty about the possible outcome and meant to help me. If Lady Camden failed in her efforts to introduce me to society, I might be sent away with a little comforting provision at my side. Perhaps token generosity was better than none at all.

"Please—I should thank them."

"Sorry, no." His eyes darted to the doorway, then back to the money. "You simply cannot do that."

"Oh." It weighed heavily in my hands. I held it back to him, but he closed my hands around it.

"Keep it, Miss Hartford. You never know when it may save you from an unexpected event."

"I will do as you say, though I cannot understand the gift."

Relief spread across his eyes. "Good. I am glad to hear it."

A silence paused between us. The curve of his sensitive lips formed around thoughts untold. He ran a hand through the too-long hair that had fallen forward, shading his brow.

"Mr. Stevens? I heard a terrible sound last night. I wondered if you did as well?"

His brows lifted. "A rather nasty shrieking sound, wasn't it?"

"The maid said to pay it no mind. I wondered if someone had been hurt—or suffers." I looked at him closely. "Can you explain?"

He rolled his eyes and paused. "I wish I could tell you that what you heard was naught but a muster of peacocks, but I would be lying." He swallowed more tea before lowering his voice. "That astoundingly annoying noise you heard was none other than Lady Camden in all her screeching glory."

"Lady Camden? I am astonished. Is she very ill?" Had she been hurt?

"Not one bit. However, she has a nasty temper when it comes to Lord Camden's stubborn ways. Who knows what he said to her that set her off."

"She shrieks like a banshee on a regular basis then? When out of temper?" I'd known an older woman in father's church who used to stomp her foot during his sermons when she disagreed with him. A loud, clacking sound of wooden soles against the flagstone floor. And a local farmer who would shout with rage when upset. His children would hide for hours beneath the church pews until he'd cooled down.

"Yes. I am sorry to say." He stood bowed with a quirk on his lips. "Let us hope that neither of us is on the receiving end of her anger, Miss Hartford, though I would not overly worry about it if I were you." He took his leave.

Sum in hand, I made my way back to my yellow room a bit bewildered. I'd not held twenty pounds in my own two hands the whole of my life. I felt as though I had indeed received an inheritance. But for whose kindness should I be grateful?

I thought it must be the Camdens, but his strange expression gave me pause. Along with the information that my hostess had an issue of anger. I made note not to cross her in any way. I hoped my resolution would not be difficult.

I needed to change my gown for luncheon and opened my small trunk. I stepped back as the lid fell away. My garments, such as they were, had been destroyed. Shredded. I lifted the pieces in my hands, one after the other, cut or ripped. Ruined. How? Why? A pair of shears had been employed, and not just that, long hand-made tears. Garment after garment ruined.

Simply destroyed.

But for one. A chemise and one nightgown remained strangely untouched. Had the intruder been interrupted?

A small knock sounded at the door before the maid entered. I turned, holding one of the shredded gowns.

"Oh my, miss." Her eyes widened and her mouth hung open. "What has happened?"

"It appears that while I was exploring the grounds, someone has made free with my things." More than made free. Mutilated—destroyed them. My heart pounded and my mouth grew dry.

A hand clasped at her throat. "I didn't do it, miss, I swear it!"

I didn't know what to think. "I'm sure you didn't." I shook my head. I knew none here besides my recent introduction to Lady Camden and Mr. Stevens. The housekeeper, too, I supposed. Who would *want* to do this? And to me. It made no sense. None at all.

I managed to get my trembling under control when I repeated the ordeal to Lady Camden not a half-hour later. She merely waved her jeweled hand at my words as though dust. Was this shrieking Lady-cousin of mine also a little mad? She didn't seem to care about my loss.

"You shall be refitted anyway, my dear. The draper is to arrive within the hour—a few ready-made gowns have been procured. Will be a simple job to adjust them to your measurements." She patted my arm. "Probably needed tossing in the rag bin, did they not?" She flashed a smile that might have been beautiful if I hadn't imagined her shrieking. "Now, let us discuss tonight's plans..."

"Tonight?" How could she dismiss me so easily? Shouldn't someone be made to pay for ruining my clothes?

"Why yes, my dear. It is New Year's Eve. Our party is this night!" Those sharp teeth gleamed again. "And the very best of my friends will be in attendance to receive you."

My heart thrummed. Tonight—not tomorrow as I had supposed.

A luncheon of cold ham and cheese, with a side of hot soup was served. I still had not been introduced to Lord Camden—perhaps he stayed away for good reason.

Lady Camden handed me a dish of olives. "You mustn't worry, dear. I see you have been raised with good manners. I daresay you know your way around a fine table?"

I nodded. We had sometimes been invited to dine at Chilham Castle. Though but a poor vicar's daughter, I was not completely ignorant of the finer things.

"Can you dance?"

"A few country dances."

"Hmmm. Never mind about that right now. This evening is supper and cards. Perhaps a little music..." Her inquiring brow rose.

"I play but little." Unless one considered the pennywhistle a worthy instrument.

"A simple tune can be most desirable." She rose from the table. "The draper will be here soon, until then, you may practice in the drawing room. After that, I daresay you'll need rest before guests arrive. You look slightly gray under your eyes." She rang a bell and the butler appeared. "Show Miss Hartford to the drawing room, Simpson."

I bit my tongue from replying. I hadn't touched a pianoforte in several months. A simple tune would be exactly what she'd hear. I rose from my chair feeling weariness about my limbs from the previous day's travel. And last night's wailing, and today's ruined clothing.

A nap couldn't come soon enough.

Chapter Four

I dared to confide in the draper's wife. This was more than I could bear alone. I recognized a kind soul as soon as I set eyes on her. She gasped at the cuts and tears.

She clucked her tongue at the ruined clothing. "Fit to make a quilt and naught else, I'm afraid." She tossed the rags back into the trunk. "All the more reason to get you these few gowns finished, and straightaway." She patted the rich folds of cloth we'd decided upon. "Do you have a key to lock the trunk?"

"I do."

"So very strange, Miss Hartford. If it happens again – which I hope it doesn't – inform Lord Camden immediately. I've never seen the like of it before!" She shook her head with another cluck of her tongue. "A maid should have certainly placed your clothing within the wardrobe by now."

I wondered if the maid had tried and found them as I had. Ruined and impossible to salvage. Did the maid perhaps think I'd destroyed my things before arriving? Lady Camden's passivity nagged. Very strange response indeed. But what could

I do? "Please don't mention it to anyone. Not yet anyway. I'd hate to create a disturbance on the brink of the New Year."

"It is too troubling, but very well." She curtsied and took the large bundle of sewing away.

In a few short hours, I would have two new day gowns, and one evening gown for tonight's entertainment. An emerald green affair without a fichu. At Lady Camden's direction, I'd been told. She certainly seemed free with her suggestions.

The seamstress and her daughter had pieced together the fabric and only had to fit them to my form. Even so, they would be at it for hours.

As for me, I'd be awake until well past midnight. A short rest was in order. I slid between the blankets and shut my eyes. Deep, deep sleep enfolded me. A true rest. Despite the strange doings that remained frayed at the edges of my mind.

I woke to a hand gripping my shoulder, shaking me awake. I gasped. What a strange place. The Yellow Room at Butterton Hall—and not my old room at the manse.

"It's nearly time, Miss Hartford." The maid's eyes widened with worry. "I'll be that punished if I don't have you turned out in time. Please, Miss."

Punished? "No need to worry, I am awake." I swung my legs over the side of the bed. "And I can be ready quickly." I tried to swipe grogginess from my eyes. "Rest assured."

In what way would she be punished? And why exactly?

"But your hair, Miss Hartford."

"My hair?"

Turns out that Lady Camden had given specific direction regarding my coiffure as well as my fichu-less gown. I stared at my reflection, concerned. My crown sported a wreath of tiny braids and a few curls dangling on either side of my face. I'd never been one to overdress my hair. Here, I appeared as a vain sort of girl—one who postured for attention.

Well. I'd allow Lady Camden this one arrangement for the holiday. As a gift to her. And then I determined to be nothing but myself.

I exited my room ready to meet the party. *Ready or not...* I took a deep breath that did little to calm. When I came to the bottom of the stairs, Mr. Stevens turned around. At his appreciative gaze, the ball of nerves in my gut instantly rotated. His hair had been trimmed and brushed back, and his black evening attire heightened the deep blue of his eyes. Too handsome.

He offered his arm. "Miss Hartford."

"Yes?"

I gulped. How silly of me. I placed my gloved hand on his strong arm and allowed him to escort me.

"You are nervous."

That wasn't a question, but a true statement. "I readily confess." My hesitancies surely showed.

"You've nothing to be concerned about." He smiled.

If that were only true. I wondered if I would find my room the way I'd left it—perfectly tidy and intact. I wasn't terribly attached to things, per se, it was only that I had so little to begin with. And the damage seemed such a waste.

Perhaps I might query this kind solicitor. "Tell me, Mr. Stevens, is there anyone here that you suspect…"

We paused before the dining room. "Yes?"

"Anyone here that could possibly suffer from madness?"

His brow lifted. "You mean, Lady Camden and her shrieking?"

"No. Not at all." Or was she perhaps a suspect? I didn't know.

"I see worry in your face." His hand pressed my elbow. "What is it?"

Dare I tell him?

The butler opened the door and my question had to wait. Before us stood a bevy of well-dressed people who turned at our late arrival. I swallowed and remembered to smile.

Lady Camden dashed forward as quickly as she could in her head finery. My eyes widened as the sparkling spectacle seemed to want to topple like the tower in Pisa. Miraculously the oddity stayed fastened. Her turban wound high, with no less than five feathers protruding from the center. I repressed the urge to giggle.

She linked her arm with mine, releasing me from the gallant Mr. Stevens. And, one by one, I was introduced to five couples and an elderly single gentleman called Dr. Rillian, one youth called Master Dawes. And, at the last, the elusive Lord Camden.

Silver-streaked hair slicked across an otherwise balding head—his bearing rather upright. He'd once been a brawny man, but age had had its cruel way.

He took my gloved hand in a prolonged hold, his eyes darting to mine and narrowing ever so little before smiling and bowing. Was as though he tried to recognize me but could not. "Charmed, Miss Hartford. Charmed. I trust Butterton Hall," his thinly mustached lip twitched, "is to your liking?"

I curtsied. "How could it not be, my lord?" The manor house was indeed pleasing, of its occupants, however, much remained to be seen and known.

"Indeed." He turned to Lady Camden and gave her his arm "We've always been very content here, haven't we, my dear?

She stiffened but delivered a bright smile. "A veritable heaven on earth." Her turban swayed as she cocked her head to one side. "You see? You were right to come to us."

Mr. Stevens approached as couples paired to enter the dining hall. He, being in trade and I being a poor vicar's daughter would enter the room last. Not that it mattered.

He offered his arm. "There are clear advantages to being at the end of the queue."

"Are there?" I laughed at his positivity.

"We always know where we are to stand and sit. We never have to figure if our place in society is any better than the one we call friend, regardless of their rank—it is, as the French might say, *automatique*." He smiled. "We can move freely with more power because we have no concerns about our standing."

"You assert that we are the tail?" I smiled.

"Moving as the head dictates, yes, but never underestimate the strength of a tail's velocity. Momentum, Miss Hartford, can incite a winning stroke."

"Momentum? I confess I am quite lost, Mr. Stevens." Did a serpent consider the muscle that propelled him forward? Or the head that profited the rest of him?

"Those of us that move about in the lower regions of good society can move about without concern that we are noticed by those who consider themselves our betters."

I was not out to win anything, by either position or momentum. However, a realization struck. Why did Lord and Lady Camden wish me here? What was their exact plan? They knew of my existence long before now.

My father had been gone for two long years without a direct word from them. The inheritance case had been in the courts longer than that. Mr. Stevens had merely suggested I come, and they'd jumped at the idea. Why? Why was I being lifted into a society I knew little about after years of no regard whatsoever?

The odd shrieks and my ruined dresses seemed nothing to the suspicion that grew in my mind. "I fear my quiet, easy days are nearing an end, Mr. Stevens. And even if I could move about as freely as you suggest and make plans for my future," I shook my head, "I will have to work hard. And very likely for my, as you put it, betters." I glanced around the room.

He pulled my chair for me, his lips lifting in a soft smile.

I was seated between him, and Dr. Rillian, who turned out to be a congenial dinner partner. Another man of trade, the sort of whom I could never tire. An open and genuine soul. Such men to me were better than the average gentleman. He reminded me greatly of my own departed father.

When it was time to turn my conversation towards Mr. Stevens, my eyes quite collided with his and his quaint chipped tooth smile. To my dismay, the school-girl blush crept up my collarbone. I dearly wished I had not listened to Lady Camden and forgone my fichu. There is a certain safety behind that light fabric tucked across my collarbones. Realizing the lack of it made me blush all the more. Next time I would more carefully consider the Lady's directives.

I opened my mouth to say something, but words were lost. Never had a handsome man so scattered my brain. How utterly discombobulating to find that I could lose control of myself in such a manner when I had always been comfortable before people of all sorts! I opened my mouth to speak, but he seemed equally at a loss.

He swallowed before saying, "Miss Hartford—" But my hostess commandeered the entire table for a little run-down of the parlor games we'd all be expected to play until the midnight hour bell chimed the New Year. I would entirely recover myself before whist.

I must. Whatever Lady Camden suggested, I was not here to attract a husband. Or was I? Good grief. The handsome solicitor had me flummoxed. As did the others.

The first round of games I played was with Lord and Lady Sherbourne, whose manners quite surprised me. They were as congenial as Dr. Rillian. I knew within minutes that Lady Sherborne and I could be good friends. I hoped occasion allowed such to happen.

Then I sat with a group of people who, as expected, felt more like strangers. Refined, very aware of the quality of their rank—and rather curious about mine, since I was seen at the end of the line with Mr. Stevens. Making them aware that I was a vicar's daughter seemed to redeem any prejudice formed as a result of their conjecture.

By eleven thirty, I'd been grouped with Mr. Stevens, Dr. Rillian, and young Matthew Dawes, who was Lady Sherborne's nephew, for a rousing game of conundrums. I had not spent a half hour with so much hilarity in many a month, and I confess, I would have won the game had not Mr. Stevens bested me. Not that I minded.

Dr. Rillian's conundrum sent us all into a laughing fit—and I imagine a near breach against propriety. Once again, Mr. Stevens began to answer the ridiculous question and would—

But the clock struck midnight, loud and clear. We all stilled, then stood as if in church. The New Year! Baby 1811 had finally arrived. The year of great changes was here and destined to move forward quickly...

Simpson handed around small glasses of wine, his deeply etched wrinkles empty of emotion. His regard – or lack thereof – for the passing of the year was undetectable.

Lord Camden held his glass high. "To all who are here, and those who are not, I toast you a goodly year with good returns—and good—"

The door slammed open and a man stumbled through. His teeth gritted as his tall form crumpled to the floor. Blood streaked his light blonde hair, dribbled about his mouth and down his cravat. He choked and gasped, reaching for his throat.

"What is the meaning of this?" Lord Camden's eyes darted about the room. "Simpson?"

The butler was missing. Dr. Rillian rushed to the stranger's side, along with Lord Camden whose face had turned red—was he angry?

"What's he trying to say?" The vicar cocked his ear.

We all did.

Unplanned, we circled the stranger as Dr. Rillian lifted the man's bloody head from the floor.

"I buried it, Camden. I buried it deep." He coughed and regained his voice. "None shall have it! No Banbury gets the last word. Not—when I gone through—the—trouble—myself." He struggled for breath. "A curse, it is. A curse—" He coughed and could not catch his breath. The next moment, he let out a great wheeze, and expired. His unblinking eyes stared at Lord Camden, and no one else.

Lord Sherborne's nephew, Matthew, grew pale, stumbled back from the group, and sank into his chair. He wiped a handkerchief across his forehead.

Dr. Rillian gently laid the man's head down as though life were indeed a sacred thing, no matter how it came to an end. "Did you know this man, my lord?"

Lord Camden backed away, pushing the notion away with the flat of his palms. "I've never seen him before in my life! I swear it!"

Why would he need to swear? Strange.

Doctor Rillain closed the man's eyes. "He seemed to know you at any rate." He positioned his arms against his side and straightened his legs. "You are quite sure? Do you need to take a closer look?"

"I certainly do not." Lord Camden's expression grew cold. "As I said." His lip twitched. "I've never seen the man before. Why he should stumble through my doors this night is beyond my understanding."

Someone behind me murmured something about Banbury. The man had buried something—deep. Who was this Banbury fellow?

Lady Camden swayed on her feet, trembling, her voice weak. "It's the Hogmanay curse." She pitched to the right and fainted before any of us could catch her.

Dr. Rillian rushed to Lady Camden—along with the good vicar's wife and Lady Sherborne.

I moved closer. "Is she well, doctor?"

Lord Camden grunted. "She's had a shock, nothing more." He tossed a glass of wine down his throat. "Nasty business to have a stranger die in your drawing room, I tell you. Especially with all this company. Nasty business."

Dr. Rillian moved from her side. "Have her carried to her room, I will follow shortly."

Lord Camden ran his hand along his chin. "See that she sleeps, won't you? A good, long time?"

The guests took their leave as quickly as they could after Lord Sherborne promised to send the magistrate. I could not blame them. The scene was not a pleasant one—a bloodied, dead man on one side of the room and a faint hostess on the other. However, I had not an inkling of how I might help the situation.

Mr. Stevens and I moved to the library where we'd been served hot coffee to calm our nerves after such an unfortunate end to the New Year's party.

I do believe the coffee livened my nerves instead of the opposite. Indeed.

"Such a shock to watch a man die like that—are you certain you don't need a glass of wine to calm yourself, Miss Hartford?"

His concern touched me. "Thank you, but no." I swallowed another gulp of the hot brew as my pulse raced all the more. I'd seen death more than a few times as I'd accompanied my father to sit bedside by the elderly in their last hours. He would administer last rites and I, with the family, would repeat the litany. *God the Father, Have mercy on your servant. God the Son, Have mercy on your servant...mercy...*

Did the deceased man know His mercy? I sincerely hoped so.

Mr. Steven's voice broke into the memory. "It is rather somber to consider, is it not?"

"Yes."

"That a man should take his last breath in the first minutes of the New Year." He poured himself another cup of coffee and added a generous portion of cream. "How ironic."

"Yes—and in such a manner." The male staff were searching the grounds for the perpetrator. I would not be able to rest easy until they were done or when the welcome sunrise lightened the many dark corners of this place.

"Not to mention he's purportedly buried something—something that has to do with the Banbury scandal. Wonder what it was."

"I heard him say that name but I know naught of scandal." So simple had my life been in Chilham. All had changed.

"No? You must not read the papers."

"Never had time for them." Though Father used to enjoy week-old news when Sir Jones was done with them.

Mr. Stevens folded his arms, sloshing the coffee on his coat. He didn't seem to notice. "I don't believe Lord Camden tells the truth about knowing the man..."

"Really? Why?" Actually, I'd had the same sense. In my experience, dying men tended toward truth-telling.

"Forgive me, Miss Hartford. I am rambling and ought not to have said such things about my employer." He seemed embarrassed.

"You may trust me, Mr. Stevens. I will not repeat your suspicion." How many times had Father and I been asked to keep silent? Confessions, revelations, fevered ramblings. "Secrecy has ever been necessary in the life of a vicar's daughter."

Relief showed on his face. "I imagine so." He leaned back and gave me a solid look—one that sought to verify the truth of my declaration. "Before the dinner, you wanted to ask me something?"

"I haven't been at Butterton Hall for very long..."

"Not more than two days yet, I think."

"Yes." I swallowed, scarcely believing all that had happened. "In that short time, the contents of my trunk—nearly all of my clothing—has been ruined. Ripped and cut—completely destroyed."

He moved to the edge of his chair. "What?"

"The maid and the draper's wife were equally astonished."

"Have you informed Lady Camden?"

"I have."

"And?"

"She waved it off as insignificant, especially as I was already receiving a new wardrobe at her expense. Today, in fact." I'd almost forgotten.

"I don't know what to think." He sat back again, as bewildered as I'd been when first discovering the ruined clothing. "And Lady Camden didn't seem to be surprised by the discovery?"

"Not in the least."

"I am confused." He shook his head. "Why would anyone want to destroy a young woman's clothing? And why were you targeted? That is troubling. Very troubling."

"Yes. It is."

"And this could not have happened before you left Chilham?"

"The trunk was with me until I arrived here..." I sipped my cooling coffee and shivered. "I suppose your clothing was never so abused since your arrival?"

"No." He looked at me with compassion. "I am sorry, Miss Hartford, that your New Year is off to such a strange beginning."

Very strange, indeed.

Simpson approached and bowed. "Doors are locked tight—no one to be found." One side of his wrinkled face twisted. "I daresay the rascal is far from here by now." He bowed yet again and left us.

I wasn't sure I'd ever be able to sleep again.

Chapter Five

I'd slept fitfully and my appetite waned despite the generous breakfast of oat porridge, sausage, and dippy eggs brought to me on an unadorned tray. The events of last night replayed like wandering ghosts in my dreams.

I queried my maid. "Mary, can you tell me—what is the Hogmanay curse?" Lady Camden's brief declaration on the subject before she fainted continued to unsettle me.

Mary backed away from me – and the question, but humored my query all the same. "The man that died—he were tall and tow-headed, weren't he?"

I nodded. The magistrate had arrived quickly with men to remove the body. None too happy to be taken from his pot of celebratory punch, mind you. His cherry-red nose shone and his cheeks ballooned as he blustered away with the inconvenience of it all. *"The Banbury scandal to reach such as village as Butterton? Unconscionable! Not to be tolerated! Especially while ringing in the New Year..."*

Mary wrung her hands. "Bein' as he be the first to cross the threshold after midnight—one such as he—well that be bad luck. Bein' as he died—well that be a curse." She swallowed, "I want to find work elsewhere, but I can't afford to leave!" A tear slipped down her cheek.

"Are you afraid of the so-called curse?"

"Aren't you?" She pressed her hands to her heart.

"No." I wasn't.

Her chin trembled. "If I were you, I'd get as far away from Butterton Hall as you could, Miss. And quickly."

"You are quite terrified." I drew close and placed a hand on her arm. "I am sure no harm will come because of that strange man's death."

"Are ye sure, Miss?"

"I am."

"But your clothing—they be—" she gulped, "torn ta shreds!"

"My gowns have been replaced." I twisted my handkerchief tightly between my fingers. "Do not fear, Mary. Instead, pray." Never mind the knot that had formed in my middle. I needed to take my own advice.

"I be doin' that non-stop." She dipped a curtsy and left me, wiping at her eyes.

I hadn't been sure of my own words. While I didn't believe the Hogmanay superstition—or curse—I did fear what man could do. What man had already done. Or woman?

Someone here perhaps suffered from lunacy. For what other reason were my gowns accosted so? I grabbed my journal and scribbled down the events as precisely as I could recall.

I laughed at the irony. Sir Jones and his dear wife would be shocked if they were to read the words. I wanted to run back to them except for the burden I would undoubtedly be. For that reason, I'd stay. For the short time it would take to find a situation. Mr. Stevens may be so kind as to help me. He'd see that I need not remain in such an odd circumstance. I'm sure of it.

But Mr. Stevens was nowhere to be found. Dark, wintry clouds spread across the sky at Butterton Hall. Snow, the house staff said, was coming. The house darkened, every corner. My "yellow" room, the darkest of them all.

In the wider spaces, a paltry gray light seeped through the great arched windows, fit for neither needlework nor reading. Candles had yet to be lit.

I didn't wonder at the economizing. Many a dark day at home, our winter's supply of candles had to be saved for Father's sermon-making. I learned to knit without looking down upon my work, however, while my knitting needles traveled with me, I had no yarn. An expense I could scarce afford at present.

I needed to do something to while away the hours before me but I couldn't sit still.

One difficult attribute I boast is my inability to wait. Once I've decided on a plan, I want to get at it. I was ready to find work and I was certain the first step was to see Mr. Stevens. I went to find him but he had left the house on some business—as Simpson had informed me. Would the snow keep him away? For how long?

No help for it. I threw on my cloak and pulled on my boots. A walk in the cold winter air would do my spirit some good. A few snowflakes wouldn't bother me. In fact, I'd relish the chance to be caught under the blessing of the downy fluff. There's something about the way soft flakes fall like so many downy feathers only to become one large blanket upon the earth.

Everything would seem pure and still—for a time at least.

I meandered about the grounds as the wind blew snow on my eyelashes. I wasn't ready to go back. No, indeed. A good romp always meant that the evening stew would taste better, and a good book all the more enjoyable. If the housekeeper could be persuaded to spare me a candle or two.

Little by little, the grounds became sugar-frosted. I hiked beyond the manicured gardens and came to an endless line of stone fencing where the snow collected in the crevices of the rocks. I don't know how long I stood there, watching the white gather heavily among the dips and rises of the valley and rock. If sheep occupied these fields, I couldn't spot them. Snow blew in heavier grey sheets and I turned to find my way back to Butterton Hall. Twas now only a faint outline.

Perhaps I had stayed out too long.

I ran—how many miles had I wandered from the Hall? The snow became a blinding force, the buildings only visible at intervals. I had no choice but to keep going in faith that I would reach shelter. All around me, snow blew. I couldn't see but one step ahead. Was this my life now? Only to know a single step without knowing where the next would take me? I began to fear. *Help, Lord.*

A freezing chill had invaded every limb. I stood in one place for a time, stomping my feet to get some feeling back into them. Finally, the snow lightened —I could see that I was near the stables—at least I thought they must be. Yes. *Thank God*. I ran towards it with all haste and with great relief, unlatched the door and went inside. I'd stay until I caught my breath and dared the final trek to the house. I wouldn't be buried alive.

The scent of sweet hay met my nose and a soft neigh sounded. Only pale light came through one tiny window. "Is anyone here?"

No one answered my call. I shouldn't wonder if the stable boy hied to the kitchen, out of this bitter cold. I shivered and peeked through the square cut into the door. The snow came in blinding sheets again. What a fool I'd been to stay outside for so long. Did the household wonder where I'd gone? Had they even noticed?

I doubted it. They'd been very much preoccupied with the stranger's shocking appearance and death—and of course, Lady Camden's health. I wouldn't be missed. However, I was very much beginning to desire a warm fire, a good book, and the forthcoming stew.

I'd wait a few more minutes and then try for the closest door. I removed my wet bonnet and shook off the snow that had gathered between the crease. My leather gloves were soaked through. I removed them too and tucked them within my cloak's pocket. Another gentle neigh of a horse reminded me that I was not alone. I made my way towards the stalls. Perhaps the horses were friendly...

I heard a scraping sound and startled. Something thunked to the ground —my head was struck, and pain cascaded down my eyes as I bent to my knees...

I don't know how long I lay on the floor of the stables before I roused. Something soft rubbed against my cheek. Like fur... I opened my eyes—pain in my head pierced. And I was cold. So very cold. The fur rubbed again and I turned my head just enough to see a small black cat. Strange company but welcome.

It mewed and rubbed its body against my arm.

"Have you been sent to warm me?" I felt as though I might never be warm again. The pain in my head intensified as the cold seeped into my bones.

I was awake for a while, then drifted into a half-wake, half-sleep state in which I dreamt I was before a large roaring fire. Father was there, reading to me. Twas a Psalm. I knew it well. "...*He restores my soul...His name's sake...yea, though I walk through the valley of the shadow of death, I will fear no evil...*"

So cold. So very cold. And the cat was gone.

Sounds broke me away from the beauty of my father's voice. How I longed to keep hearing it! *Speak again, father. Continue your words...* I recounted the rest of them. I mumbled them. *Join me, Father.*

Hooves stamped. A man hummed a tune.

Strong arms gathered me. *Father? Was he here?* Pain pressed. I uttered the rest of the following words, "Thy rod and thy staff, they comfort me. Thou preparest a table in the presence of mine enemies: thou anointest my head with oil..."

A hand brushed my forehead "Looks like your head does need anointing. Good heavens, what has happened to you?"

I recognized the voice and groaned as new pain shot through my head.

"Can you hear me, Miss Hartford? Can you tell me what happened?"

The psalm wasn't finished. The arms about me tightened. What were the next words? *Surely goodness and mercy will follow me all the days of my life...*

"Why are you in the stables on a day like this?"

Chills scampered along my body as I fully woke. "Mr. Stevens..." I blinked to see his handsome face, his deep blue eyes narrowing as they sought answers.

"You are bleeding," He pressed a handkerchief to my temple. "You need a doctor at once."

I didn't argue.

"Did you have an accident with one of the horses?"

I didn't know. I wiped a hand across my eyes as he lifted me from the ground and carried me from the stables. The snow had diminished to tiny, aimless flecks. "Something hit me. I don't know... I don't know..." I'd been about to greet the horses—had I made it to the stalls?

He tightened his hold "Be still. Perhaps you shouldn't try to talk just yet."

He carried me into the kitchens—the pungent scent of onion and garlic snapped my senses fully awake. "Make way, you! Here, clear the path."

"What's this?" A woman's voice rose among the clatter of work. "She be better off in the keepin' room, Mr. Stevens." The cook. She wiped her palms on her long apron. "Here, set her here on the cot. Not used yet, mind you. Stable boy had the sense to sleep in the house tonight."

The sudden warmth of the room burned. Every part of me felt the heat. A high fire flickered in the grate. The cook scooted the cot directly in front of it. Mr. Stevens lowered me but didn't release his hold.

"What she be doin' out in this weather?"

Mr. Steven's voice vibrated through his chest. "Send for the doctor, Mrs. Watts. Quick, now."

"Yes, sir. Should I see that Lord and Lady Camden are informed?"

"I will see to that myself."

He shifted against the wall as another round of shivers beset me.

"You there! Bring hot bricks. And tea." He tugged at the wet cloak and pulled it away from my body. "Here—the blanket's rather thin. I'll see another one is brought to you." He brushed wet strands of hair from my eyes. "Hold on, Mis Hartford."

"I thought my father had come..." How close I'd been to seeing him again. At least in my dreams.

"You must have been knocked cold."

Cold was an understatement. "I went looking for you earlier."

"Is everything alright?" He shook his head. "No—I can see that it isn't." He looked upon my wound with observant eyes. "I'll feel better when the doctor can take a look. Hurt anywhere else?"

"I don't think so." I shivered again as maids appeared with hot bricks, tucking them about me as they covered my form with more blankets.

"I must see to my horse. Stay put, Miss Hartford. I will return." His blue eyes were firm. I daren't disobey him.

Had anyone ever been so gallant towards me? Not that I could recall. And what a pitiful sight I must have been.

True to his word, Mr. Stevens returned quickly, placing a large mug of tea in my hands. I sipped ever so slowly. My arms had become pudding. So very weak.

He threw off his overcoat and pulled a chair close to me. "Looks like a pitchfork fell from a broken peg as you passed beneath it. What odd timing." He looked at my head. "Has no one seen to your wound?"

"Just here, Mr. Stevens. If ya be so kind as to allow me to help." The grim-faced housekeeper who had escorted me from Chilham.

"Thank you, Rothy." He moved to the other side of the cot while the woman set a steaming bowl of water and clean linen beside me.

She began to gently pat my head. Blood came away. Had I been knocked so very hard? "If I may ask, how is Lady Camden today?"

The housekeeper's eyes darted to mine, then away again. "I know naught but that she keeps to her bed."

"Know you anything more about the stranger?"

I shouldn't have asked. Her teeth gritted together in a straight line. An expression I knew well. "Better he be dead." She dropped the bloody cloth into the bowl and left me. How could one wish another soul dead unless he was truly evil?

Mr. Stevens must have been thinking along the same lines. "She knew him."

I took another sip of tea.

Mr. Stevens leaned forward, hands on knees. "And what, may I ask, were you doing out in this bitter cold? You say you were looking for me?"

"Did I?" I wondered when. "I do seek some counsel, however, I merely wanted some fresh air. I wandered too far from the house before the storm worsened. Made my way to the stables—and then I heard a noise…"

"Must have been the pitchfork falling."

"Must have been."

A voice shouted through the halls and down to the kitchens. "I'll whip the irresponsible boy who put our houseguest in danger!"

A small form scampered from the kitchen followed by a cat. I faintly recalled the animal. There'd been a cat with me, nestled at my side. I was sure of it.

"Where is he?" Lord Camden knocked an empty bucket from the table.

Cook stirred a kettle of simmering onion, hardly responding to the rash temper. "I've not seen him, my lord."

A lie.

A fist smacked into the palm of his hand. "Hmph." Lord Camden sauntered to my cot. "Dr. Rillian will attend you within the hour." He clicked his teeth. "In the future, keep to the house and not go wandering off."

Such kindness. He left us without even a wish for improved health.

"My apologies, Miss Hartford. Lord Camden can be rather rude."

"I hate to detain you." I struggled to lift the cup to my lips. My body still hadn't returned to normal. "I'm sure you have a great deal to do."

"Nonsense. You're wounded. I'm not leaving your side until Dr. Rillian arrives."

In truth, I didn't want to be left alone. Wanted him to stay nearby. The house staff buzzed around the kitchens as though nothing had happened. No one seemed to care one whit about me.

I looked at Mr. Stevens and his hopeful smile. Never had I found myself befriended by such a handsome man. The warmth that flooded my veins and boosted my pulse had nothing to do with the hot brick at my feet.

Chapter Six

"You'll need stitches, my dear." Dr. Rillian's hands had been gentle, his expression wary. "Do you give me permission to sew?"

I nodded as pain burst around my eyes.

"It will leave a scar, I'm afraid." His concern showed.

"A scar?" Not only my life but my visage would forever change. "Please do as you see fit, Doctor."

Mr. Stevens spoke up. "I assure you. Such a small alteration will not detract from your beauty, Miss Hartford."

"I am not concerned." I gulped at his compliment. "I thank you for your kind words." Indeed. His own chipped tooth only added interest to his attractive features. My heartbeat quickened. How dare I entertain such thoughts?

The many minutes of careful stitching felt like an eternity. Because I'd been so cold, Dr. Rillian didn't think it wise to calm my nerves with wine. The use of opiates was out of the question. Mr. Stevens nestled my hands within his. No other gentleman of rank would stay to comfort someone of my low status.

When I looked into the mirror, I saw a jagged line that trailed from my crown to my right eyebrow. Skin swelled around the stitches and grew taut. A new hairstyle might well be in order...

"Now, let us see to the other wound." Dr. Rillian pulled hair away from behind my ear. "My, my."

"I must have fallen after I was hit." The pain increased as the stitches pulled, and Dr. Rillian's touch to my other wound sent fire down my neck. I subdued a yelp.

"Hmm..."

I closed my eyes as I felt a hand gather mine into his own. Mr. Stevens. Would that everyone had such a person to help them through a trial.

"No more sewing, but you'll need to keep the area clean and bandaged."

Another ordeal as he spread ointment into the wound and wrapped cloth tightly around my head. Dr. Rillian stood. "I will pray for you, Miss Hartford, and will call upon you tomorrow morning." He bowed. "A private word with you, Mr. Stevens."

They moved to the corner of the room. I couldn't hear their mumbling. Did it have to do with me? Then Mr. Stevens spoke. "You're saying that she was purposefully struck?"

"I know wounds. And I know when bodily harm has been done to another. Look out for her, Mr. Stevens. Since last night's escapade..."

I heard no more as they stepped from the room.

Lunacy does live here. Someone attacked me. Why? My body tingled with warmth, my head with pain, my heart with fear... A quiet terror gnawed.

Cook brought a tray of the stew I'd craved all day. I wasn't sure I could eat.

Mr. Stevens, once again, positioned by at my side. "I know it hurts, but you need sustenance, Miss Hartford. You must keep up your strength."

A rogue tear slipped down my face and I swiped it away.

He handed me his starched handkerchief. "Not the way you imagined the New Year to begin, is it?"

"Not exactly."

He handed me a heaped spoon. I took a bite, chewing slowly.

"When you've recovered, I have something to show you."

"And what would that be? You sound a bit mysterious."

"I do, rather."

"Can't you tell me now?"

"Not while your head hurts."

"I see." More bad news. Lady Camden desired me far from Butterton Hall. Of course. I had decided the very thing for myself already. "When I have recovered, I should like some assistance to find a situation elsewhere."

"A situation?"

"I believe I've mentioned it before."

"On this, Miss Hartford, I beg you to wait." The cook handed him his tray of food. "Do you mind if I join you?"

I shook my head. "You haven't left my side. I thank you for your kindnesses this afternoon." I might have died had he not discovered me and sought my immediate care.

"It's been my honor to do so." He bowed his head, his lips a gentle smile.

An hour later, he carried me once again, as though I weighed nothing, to my yellow chamber, taking each step carefully as my head pounded like a workman's hammer. He settled me onto my bed and left with regret upon his face.

"I hate to leave you. Are you sure you will be alright?"

"There is nothing to do but rest." And face my fears. I'd been attacked. Nothing would change that. He didn't realize that I'd heard.

"I shan't be far. Send for me should you require anything."

"I thank you. Good night." Would he look out for me as Dr. Rillian suggested?

Two maids had been sent to assist me into my nightgown. A cup of hot chocolate had been sent, courtesy of Lady Camden, whose own fears about the Hogmanay curse only grew with the news of my near demise. My maid, Mary, was nowhere to be seen. Had she flown?

"Where is Mary?" I dared to ask.

"No one's seen her since this morning, Miss."

"She's gone missing?"

"An' the housekeeper's in a right foul mood, that one."

I wondered if she ever wasn't in a foul mood. Mary had been terrified this morning. And now she was gone. I prayed she fled to her home, wherever that might be... Hopefully far from here.

Something leapt upon my bed and I stifled a scream. The cat! Twas only the cat. Must have followed the maids within and been trapped inside my room. I was glad not to be entirely alone. When my mother had died, Father procured a kitten for me—whose antics livened the manse for many a year.

This animal's black fur boasted a glossy sheen, a chunk was missing from one ear and his tail looked like it had been broken once upon a time. The beast had no doubt won a fight or two and lived to meow about it. He slipped to my side and purred. I stroked his fur as he settled in.

Such a little companion sent to combat my loneliness. No match for Mr. Stevens, but still appreciated.

I drank the cocoa and became drowsy. Sleep would be a remedy for all that was twisted and tangled within my mind. No, I didn't believe the Hogmanay curse. But I did believe that lives could be cursed. I would not partake of such darkness. No, indeed. Whatever was happening at Butterton Hall—someone desired to be rid of me. Why? I was of no consequence to anyone, never have been...

I woke in the middle of the night with throbbing pain. Counting sheep wasn't going to work, so I recited as many Scripture passages as I could recall and moved on to Shakespeare. I refused to let my fears get the better of me and keeping my mind busy seemed the best solution.

That is until a noise shuffled at my door. The cat jumped to the floor and scampered atop my desk, tipping over a glass of quill pens.

My recitations halted as my heart quickened. Had my attacker returned to finish the job? Would I die this night? If only there were a way to bolt this room from within, I might have kept myself safe. My throat closed when I tried to swallow, my ears roared.

I slowly crept from bed, threw a shawl around my shoulders, and found the fire poker. At least I had something. I halted. The shuffling had stopped. I took a deep breath and a silent moment passed—when the sound began again. *Dear God, what should I do?*

I gripped my weapon. My door was unlocked, why did they hesitate? Truly, if I was the target I would have already been struck down. Dr. Rillian must be wrong... the pitchfork had fallen from the peg. That was all. He'd imagined things.

In a sudden move, I decided to open the door to my fate. I'd knocked a dog away from me many years ago. I could do the same again with as much gusto. I flung it open with the fire poker held high. I wanted to look as menacing as possible.

I gasped. There, hunkered on the ground was a man in shirtsleeves and an unbuttoned vest. "Mr. Stevens?" He looked quite disheveled.

"Miss Hartford? What are you doing up?" Surprise lit his bright eyes as they traveled to my weapon.

I lowered the poker. "What are you doing by my door." Not my assailant. Surely not.

He stood. "Forgive me, did I wake you?" He whispered.

"You haven't answered my question." Was he being evasive?

He hesitated before buttoning his vest. "It appears I must explain myself. Do forgive me." He retied his cravat. "I was attempting to rest, albeit uncomfortably."

"That is not an explanation. And why exactly in this spot?" Dr. Rillian's words came back to me. He'd tasked Mr. Stevens with my protection. Could that be the reason? "I heard what you and the doctor talked about."

His head jerked up and his eyes assessed mine. "I am sorry you did." He looked up and down the narrow hall. "Strange events are occurring in this place and I couldn't live with myself if anything else happened to you." He loosened the knot at his neck. "It is my doing that you are here in the first place."

I set the poker in the doorway and touched my head. The pounding had grown with the fear—and while the fear had vanished at Mr. Steven's words, the pounding had not.

He grimaced with regret. "I've frightened you. I am so sorry."

"No—well, yes." I reached for his hand and squeezed. "It is good to have a friend while I am here." A friend and a protector.

He motioned towards the bed. "You need to rest."

"And you also need yours."

"I will take it here, outside your door."

"That isn't necessary…"

"I believe it is."

"What if the peg merely broke as you originally thought?"

He countered. "And what if a little sprite dashed into your trunk and shredded your garments on a whim?" He shook his head. "Allow me this. I promise to leave before the maids return." A brow rose.

"Very well, then." My nerves did calm at the thought of his presence on the other side of the door. "I bid you goodnight. Again."

"Here." He reached and adjusted my bandage. "The knot was slipping. Have a care, Miss Hartford. Perhaps these events are truly nothing. But if they aren't..." He took another deep breath. "Next time you decide to go for a walk, wait for me to go with you. I would be truly honored."

I nodded. I wouldn't be here much longer. Walks about the estate weren't likely to happen again.

I closed my bedroom door, crawled back into bed, and slept in an exhausted stupor. I slept so long that I didn't hear Lady Camden's shrieking the next morning when she discovered that her favorite horse had disappeared from the stables. I slept in blessed ignorance until the sun bid adieu at half past five o'clock and the candles had been lit. My visitor cat was nowhere to be seen.

Mr. Stevens told me about the day's issues over coffee in the library. Propriety dictated that we never be alone together. The doors were wide open, and a maid worked across the room dusting books, one volume at a time. However, we didn't wish to be overheard. He leaned close. "Someone has stolen the beast."

"Perhaps my attacker?"

"Possibly."

My headaches had eased to a throbbing dull tug. Of this I was grateful.

Mr. Stevens swallowed a gulp of coffee. "Lord Camden doesn't believe that you were attacked, or that his horse was stolen. No, indeed. He says that you must have unlatched the stall while you were nosing about—and then left the door open."

So it was my fault? I shook my head. "But that isn't so!"

"I know." He set his empty cup down. "I took care of my horse after helping you to the kitchen yesterday. The stalls were properly bolted. I made sure of it."

"How strange."

"Indeed it is."

Simpson strutted through the library and bowed. "Dr. Rillian to see you, Miss."

His brows rose. "How timely. Perhaps he can persuade Lord Camden to take these events more seriously."

"I should think your word to be enough." I certainly believed it was.

Mr. Stevens stood. "You could assume such since my father and I represent him." He offered his hand. "Dr. Rillian, you've come."

The kind man smiled as they shook hands. He set his bag on the chair beside me. "How is my patient? Headache bearable yet?"

"It is."

He checked my stitches and unwound the bandage. "I'm sorry I couldn't come sooner. I had another patient in need of ministrations."

"As you see, I am no worse for the wear." The coffee had soothed my headache.

"Ah, my dear, you are young! You have a long way to go before that happens." He laughed. He redressed my wound and left instructions for my maid.

Mr. Stevens poured a fresh cup of coffee. "Here, doctor. You must have had a cold ride from Goodwyn Abbey."

"I thank you." He drank it black and hot. "Given you thought to what we discussed yesterday?" He waited for an answer.

"I have. You must know that Miss Hartford overheard us."

"Oh dear. Well. Best she knows to be on her guard." He looked at me. "You saw no one in the stables?"

My turn to be questioned. "None." I yawned, though I had slept for several hours, exhaustion beset me.

Dr. Rillian looked about the room before settling back on Mr. Stevens. "None of this sits well with me, Ewan."

His name was Ewan... Finally, I knew.

"Is there any way you can release yourself from representing Camden? Business that has anything to do with Banbury—oof, man. It's going to get ugly. I'd hate to see the good name of Stevens and Stevens ruined by association."

Ewan's back stiffened. "I thank you for your concern but I have no choice in the matter. As the junior partner, I must do my father's bidding—or be out of a job."

"Well." The doctor slapped his knee. "'Tis the society we live in. Most of us must, without regard to our personal desires, fulfill the designs of our good parents. Hoping they are good, that is."

"Did you work for your father?" He asked.

"I? Nay. Didn't have a father." He set his cup down and stood. "Learned my trade from a ship's doctor, and more so, from the many leg and torso surgeries made necessary by the American War of Independence." He looked at me. "Pardon me, Miss Hartford. I hope I haven't caused distress."

"Please, do not concern yourself."

Ewan rose as well. "I will do my job to the best of my ability. That is all I can do."

The doctor tapped his nose. "Ah, not all, my boy. Not at all." He chuckled. "What happens when your work crosses a boundary where it shouldn't?"

"Should my work entail crossing the law, both moral and physical, then I might find myself the richer for leaving such crossings to those who don't mind being compromised. I'm not afraid to lose as a result of doing right. But you must know, Dr. Rillian, that my father would do the same should it ever come to that."

"Well done, Ewan." He winked. "I will pray that your..." he coughed, "representation of Lord Camden in the Banbury case does not reap the ramifications of the offender. Assuming Camden is guilty—or not?" He sighed. "Time will tell. Always does."

He patted my hand, his reassuring smile reaching his eyes, "Should you find yourself in trouble, you can trust Ewan." He turned to leave but paused. He waved us behind the shelving, away from the maid's eyes. "I forgot to give you these." He pulled from his satchel two daggers. "Courtesy of Lord Sherborne. Should you both need protection."

A matched set. My stomach squeezed. Surely, we would not need to use them. Why did everyone fear so much? Why did I? How exactly does one hold a dagger?

"Oh," He pulled a message from his medical bag and handed it to me. "This is from Lady Sherborne." He nodded. "I'll be off now, send word if you develop a fever. Otherwise, I believe you'll mend well. My prayers remain with you."

Dr. Rillian left us alone, once again. I struggled for words. "Should we not leave this place if we must carry a weapon? Would that not be safer?" I shuddered at the sharp weapon I held, afraid I might accidentally cut myself. What damage it could cause...

"I cannot." He pocketed his as I tucked mine securely, out of sight beneath my shawl.

"I have nowhere to go." No manse to return to. No other family...

"Should it come to that, Miss Hartford..." Words failed both of us. His eyes grazed mine. "I have every confidence that..."

"Cousin Jane?" Lady Camden sent her frantic query across the room. "Tell me you are here?"

I pulled a book from the shelf and slipped from the hiding place. What would she think to find Mr. Stevens and I alone in such a manner? "I am here."

"Oh, look at you!" She pressed a hand to her heart. "To think that a dreadful curse should touch my dearest cousin..."

Dearest cousin? Not for the first time did I doubt her sincerity. We had no history together. Yet a few short nights beset with danger, and I had become so exceedingly dear... Why?

Chapter Seven

Twelfth Night had come. My first week at Butterton Hall would conclude with yet another party around the dining table, despite my misgivings. The last celebration had triggered dreadful events. But Lady Camden refused to be dissuaded. The party must go on.

"Perhaps my dear, by following tradition, we might lessen the curse." She shuddered. "Thank goodness I burned the Christmas greenery before your arrival or we might suffer yet more!" She dabbed her nose with a handkerchief. "Most of the villagers would have us burn the greenery this night, but that is ludicrous."

"Indeed?" I thought of the yew and rosemary that still hung on the newel post in the old foyer. She must not know it remained. In Chilham, many villagers kept greenery hanging until Candlemas. But we certainly weren't in Chilham anymore.

What must it be like to live as though bad luck lurked around each corner? Or to suffer an imagined curse that caused more damage by fanning fears that plagued those who believed in its foolishness? Poor Lady Camden. Was there not enough evil in this world that she must add to it?

Twas a smallish party that gathered, including the vicar and his wife, along with a pair of older gentlemen I'd not met. I suspected the inclusion of the vicar had a lot to do with Lady Camden's desperation for the curse to be lifted. If anyone could accomplish this, a vicar might. This particular man had the sort of heavy hand that might be able to put a stop to the nonsense. His rich laugh alone would chase away the ghosts that haunted Butterton's hallways. I wondered what he would say next.

Given my limited options, I'd dressed in the same green evening gown, but this time, trimmed my hair to cover the ghastly stitches.

Mr. Stevens bowed. "You look well, Miss Hartford."

"I thank you." I took his offered arm as we made our way to the dining table. "You've been very busy these past few days. Is there much to do?"

He nodded. "A great deal."

He still had not shown me—or told me what he mentioned the day of my attack. I would ply him after the party. The Camdens agreed that there'd been no attacker, so I determined to play the same game. Whether I'd been assaulted or not, I knew I must leave this *rapturous* place soon. With the twenty pounds of comfort to help me on my way.

I didn't desire my existence to be wholly dependent on how well I wielded the little blade strapped to my leg. I desired to live in a home where I might do some good. Something true and real. Not constantly fear for my safety.

Dinner was served and eaten, then the Twelfth Night cake and mince pies were before us. Lady Camden was too bright. An artifice of joy, her smile lacked true contentment.

"You must all partake. You simply must."

Had tradition slumped into superstition as well? I confess I was in a mood and not one to celebrate. I bit into the rich concoction of currant, spice, and lemon—rich and glorious. Had been years since I'd tasted the like. Yet it could not penetrate the mild despair that hung like a cloud about me.

The vicar seemed to swallow his mince pie whole. "The last hours of Christmas should always include such divine pudding as this."

His wife laughed.

He continued. "Indeed. Christ came that we might have life lived to the full! Abundantly, he says!"

Lord Camden raised his glass. "I concur."

"Though not in gluttony." The vicar laughed.

Lady Camden bent her head. "Of course not."

"Might I beg for another healthy slice of cake, Lady Camden?" The vicar grinned. "As Jonathan in the Good Book would say, 'see how my eyes have brightened?' Your cook's recipe is unmatched."

"Indeed, you may!" She motioned to the servant.

The request seemed to make her happier. I watched as she downed a third glass of wine. She would need help up the stairs if she swallowed more.

The vicar pointed his fork in my direction. "Life lived to the full, Miss Hartford. What say you?"

He referred to verses that talked of a thief coming to steal, kill, and destroy. A stark contrast to Jesus who came that His sheep might not only have life, but a life of abundance. Father loved preaching from John.

I responded. "If one would but follow the Shepherd that walks through the appropriate gate and not the thief who entered another way, one might be kept safe from destruction." I refrained from noting that gorging on cake was not exactly what was meant by an abundant life.

"Ah, you are right. Fear could be stifled so long as one stayed focused on Christ." His gaze penetrated. "Each sheep need only stay close to the Shepherd. Here, we find safety."

"Indeed." Would that my gaze never left Him. I understood clearly. A thief had assaulted me. Tried to destroy me. "Even if..." I couldn't finish aloud. Even if I should go to the grave, goodness and mercy would follow me. He would preserve my soul, regardless of my life here on earth.

"Yes, Miss Hartford." He nodded, "Even if."

No matter what, I must keep my gaze on my Shepherd. Even if...

Abundance would come regardless.

A hand slipped into mine beneath the table, his comforting warmth pressed close. Ewan held my hand tightly. I glanced at his plate and risked a quick look at him. He offered a soft smile.

I think he knew in that moment, that despite my brave words, fear threatened like a wolf. He would be my guardian for as long as I remained. For that, I was very glad.

Lord Camden rose. "Enough of this catechizing, vicar. Let us to our port."

The evening progressed, ending ultimately with our guests departing—without a stranger stumbling through the door, dying before our eyes. Much to Lady Camden's relief.

We gave a final wave goodbye as Lady Camden turned to me. "Perhaps the curse is lifted now." She patted my arm. "Soon, we may see about introducing you to some worthy gentleman, you may count on it!"

Oh my. She still wanted to be my matchmaker? And apparently without my input or consent. I hoped to be long gone by then.

"I can see how interested you are." Her eyes glimmered. "I'll have hot chocolate sent to your room."

"I do believe I will read in the library for a while. It is still early." I sent a look to Mr. Stevens, who inclined his head. He understood.

She nodded. "Very well." She and her maid left —Lord Camden had rushed away as soon as they were across the threshold. Who knew where he'd gone off to? Gentlemen may do as they like. I thought it both odd and rude.

We stepped into the library where a low fire had been left. Simpson followed us with a bow. "Shall I see the chocolate delivered here, Miss Hartford?"

"Yes, please."

He bowed again and left.

Mr. Stevens and I sat in front of the hearth, gazing into the flames.

"I do wish your assistance with finding a situation." I folded my hands. "Please."

"I know that you do. I beg you to wait."

"Must I?"

"It may be profitable if you do."

"You know I do not expect to win the inheritance."

"Yes, as you told me. But what if I told you that I found something potentially helpful?" He tented his fingers casually beneath his lips. "I found papers that tie your family name—to this estate. To Butterton Hall. What if I told you that the main reason I had for bringing you here was to correct an old wrong and see Butterton Hall placed into rightful hands?" He reached out to me. "Your hands, Jane Hartford..."

"But the inheritance—the one tangled up in court—"

"Is still hopelessly tangled and might be for a long time."

We paused our conversation as a maid delivered the cups of steaming chocolate.

"I don't understand you, Mr. Stevens."

"I've been staying here for a few months, going through papers, ledgers, family records. I was tasked to find anything that would help the case in court. Just before Christmas, I stumbled upon a letter dated some fifty years ago, bearing the Hartford name. I looked into it. Even paid a visit to the church for records of marriages and baptisms. It very much appears that the family line of inheritance was manipulated to your detriment."

I shook my head. "Are there not laws to protect against such?"

"There are laws aplenty." He released my hands. "But once in a while, important events either go unrecorded or as in this case, a death was assumed."

"I still don't understand."

"Butterton Hall should have gone to your great grandfather as he was the eldest. Only he was presumed dead and the estate went to his brother. Lady Camden's grandfather."

"Presumed dead..."

"It very much appears that your great-grandfather didn't die, but changed his name."

"Why would he?"

"I don't know. But what I do know is that while there is a death certificate, there is no grave."

"Perhaps he died at sea."

"No, Miss Hartford. Jane, if I may..."

I nodded.

"The letter points to his suffering from dementia."

I was so very confused. "And how do you know that this Hartford mentioned is the same man as my great-grandfather?"

"Too much of a coincidence, don't you think? That you and Lady Camden are in line for the same inheritance? That being the case, how is it that she is at risk of losing that one when she easily gained Butterton? The win should be a foregone conclusion." He sipped his chocolate. "My father sent me to go over the documents so that the case could be quickly settled—at Lord Camden's bidding, of course."

"Let me try to understand. You believe, following the appropriate family line that my great-grandfather gave his birthright to his younger brother, faked his death, and went on to live a more common life?"

"A birthright not legally given up. The law must recognize the true lord of the estate—or lady in this case."

It was too much to take in.

"I have not revealed these facts to Lord and Lady Camden…but…"

"Must you?"

"I cannot allow a lie to prevail."

"You are a man of integrity, I can see that."

"Thank you."

"I do not want Butterton Hall."

"Do you not? Think of the good that you can do here."

"I can think of it." Sir Jones and his wife came to mind. "But to disrupt a chain of events none of us can help…"

"You would be disrupting a dreadful outcome and introducing a better kind of society and a far more caring lady." He smiled. "The world needs more people like you."

My face heated at his compliment. His words challenged me.

"So, you see, you must stay. Lord Camden has his dealings with Banbury to clear up. Then I feel it my duty to set this aright."

I felt as though a boulder had been set on my shoulders. How furious the Camdens would be if Mr. Stevens followed through on his plan. "I beg you to drop it, sir. I did not come here to set down my relatives, nor to take place as a lady."

"I understand. In a few weeks, I will take the information to my father in London. I will take no action until and unless he advises." He opened his empty hands. "There is a legal death certificate, after all. Regardless that he lived, married, and had children under a different name, it may not matter to the crown. However, if there's anything the crown values, it's direct bloodlines."

"And you are certain that Lord and Lady Camden are ignorant of your findings?"

"I thought not." His expression grew serious. "But after the events of the last week, I am not so certain."

"How do you mean?"

He pulled a scrap of fabric from his waistcoat. "Someone doesn't want you here." He handed me the fabric. It was mine. From one of my ruined gowns. "I found it on the rug in Lord Camden's study."

Urgency filled me. "All the more reason I must go." Anxiety again urged me to exit. I stood but his hand stalled me.

"Believe it or not, you are safer here than on your own where anyone can get to you." He blinked and stood to face me. "I will sleep at your door for as long as it takes. You needn't be afraid."

"I'm trying ever so hard to not fear."

He closed his eyes, then lifted his hand to my shortened length of hair that covered the stitches. His blue eyes perused my wound before setting his lips there in a brief kiss. "I won't let anyone else hurt you."

If only I could dare to completely trust.

Chapter Eight

I couldn't sleep. No matter how hard I tried. I took some comfort knowing that Mr. Stevens was positioned outside my door. Pleasant thought. What he'd said earlier that evening befuddled my ability to think straight.

He must be wrong. And even if he wasn't, I had no inclination to pursue ownership of this rambling residence. Yet his words pressed. *Think of the good you can do here...* Many options stretched out before me.

Lord? Do you want me to stay? Your will be done. Yes, Your will be done...

His kiss to my wound...so tender. Another sweet memory. The man had been utterly good to me since I'd arrived. I was drawn to him. But I needed to be careful not to mistake his kindness for something it wasn't.

I crawled from my covers, shivering from the frozen night, and donned my robe. I built up the fire, lit a candle, and began to scratch out the previous days' events and intrigues in my journal. I paused. Perhaps I ought not be so bold with my conjecture. I set my pen down.

If anyone could enter my room and go through my things—and read it, what then? But what did I have to hide? Nothing – and everything.

A creak sounded and I jolted. My door. Opening slowly. I hoped to see only one man's face. Mr. Stevens slipped within and held a finger to his lips. "Quiet," he whispered. He held his dagger, blade from its sheath. "Someone is coming. Put out your candle."

I did as told, terror ripping through me. Yet again.

"Hide in the wardrobe. Quickly."

I hesitated as he held the door open. Footsteps shuffled at my door. I hid and he followed.

We hunched in the wide space below the shelving just as my door clicked open. My heart pounded, my breath came in spurts.

Heavy footsteps turned about my room. A man's voice murmured, "Where has she got to?" He spat an expletive.

Nausea swirled. The voice belonged to Lord Camden.

I was not safe here. If he discovered my hiding place, I could die. Mr. Stevens and I could both die. I held my breath for what seemed an eternity. Mr. Stevens took my hand and squeezed. He would protect me.

Moments later, Lord Camden left the room, his steps trailing off. Mr. Stevens bade me stay put until he felt it safe for me to exit the cramped space. First to the floor, he gave me his hand and pulled me out. I trembled, and not from the cold.

He pulled me to his chest and held me, whispering into my hair. "You were right. You cannot stay here."

"What did he want?"

"I wish I knew."

I think we both suspected the worst. He wanted to kill me. I looked into Mr. Steven's eyes and saw the unavoidable truth there. Why else had I been placed in a little used portion of the house? Far from anyone else.

Mr. Stevens spoke first. "He knows. Don't know how—I didn't tell him, but somehow, he knows about the family line. All of the questions and confusion. And you are most definitely in the way." He rubbed at his tired eyes. "And I'm the one that brought you here—right in the middle of this strange danger." He cupped my chin in his hands. "I am so sorry, Jane." He closed his eyes. "I will mend this. I will see you to safety."

All I could do was nod. And hope.

He stayed until the maids stirred. The slow hours before dawn had been sickening. He rested against the door from within my room and I packed a small bag. I would leave unnoticed—had to, somehow.

"You need to be seen this morning, act as though everything is normal. He must not suspect that you know he entered your room." He sheathed his dagger. "I will send word to the Sherborne's. They will help."

"Will they not think me ludicrous?"

"You don't know the Sherborne's very well. I assure you. They will help us."

I nodded. At this juncture, I had no other option than to trust.

"Until I come for you, meander about. Stay in areas where the household is at work. No one will touch you, I'm certain."

"I am afraid."

"You are also brave. Unselfish. Kind..." He took my hand. "I've never met another woman like you, Jane..."

Like me? A plain, poor vicar's daughter? I lowered my eyes and curtsied. "Thank you for guarding my life with your own."

"I would do nothing else." He bowed and left.

The first week of the new year had been both intriguing and terrible. Today, I would leave it behind and restart a new, fresh week somewhere else. Or I would be killed.

I did as told and spent the morning near the housekeeping. I stepped into the morning parlor with a book in hand—knowing full well that I wouldn't be able to focus on the words. My nerves were frayed and I jumped at sudden noises.

I'd just settled into a chair when the door opened. Lord Camden, the last man I wanted to see. My hand went to my throat.

"Leave us, Jenny." The maid did as told and left her steaming scrubbing bucket at the cold hearth. Sweat glistened across his face. He jerked a handkerchief from his pocket and swiped at his forehead. "I've been looking for you everywhere, my dear!"

He paced before me. Spots danced before my eyes. Would I faint?

"I thought for sure you'd got yourself lost in the wood." He clicked his teeth. "Lady Camden would never forgive me if anything else happened to our esteemed guest."

"Indeed." What was he babbling about?

"Indeed. Yes, indeed!" He sat down, pulled leather gloves off his hands, and tossed them down in a smack. "You weren't in your bed last night."

How dare he? I gasped. "Sir."

"Scamper down to the kitchens, did you? Hungry, perhaps?" He eyed me like a naughty child caught stealing sweets.

I didn't answer. What could I say? I'd been hiding in a wardrobe, fearing for my life.

He clapped a hand to his face. "Forgive me, dear, I must sound like a rogue for saying I entered your room. But a message was sent that you were gravely ill. Simpson brought it to me himself."

Simpson? But why? "How strange. As you see, I am well."

"Yes, yes. Thank God." He observed me over the thin mustache. "Someone has played a nasty trick upon me, dash it." He picked up his gloves again and lay them across his knee. "I'll have to talk with them. Again."

I gripped my book, confused. Should I believe him? "Again, Lord Camden?"

"Mmm," he grunted. "Simpson must be losing his mind." He slapped his knee. "I'll not see another foul event happen upon these grounds."

And yet he had declared my wounds the result of an accident... or did he mean to put me at ease? To keep me here? Why? My heartbeat quickened. I carried my dagger, but would I be able to stop shaking sufficiently to reach it? Or were we completely mistaken about the man? I didn't know who or what to believe anymore.

Mr. Stevens walked in—and paled when he saw who sat across from me. He recovered quickly. "Miss Hartford." He bowed. "Lord Camden. Good morning. I have a document that requires your signature and seal, if you will."

"Would that be for the letter of denial?"

"It would."

"Very well. If you'll excuse us, Miss Hartford. I am glad you are not missing," he coughed, "or gravely ill." He gave me an odd smile.

I inclined my head. "Good morning, Lord Camden. Mr. Stevens."

Ewan sent me a questioning glance as he left the room. *Ewan*... if only I might say his name as he says mine. Why did I feel so drawn to a man I'd only known for a week? A near stranger and yet I felt I could trust him with my life. Which is exactly what I was doing. Even if he was gravely mistaken about my inheritance.

Hours passed before Mr. Stevens and I could meet again. Tea had been served in the library at four o'clock, and Lady Camden conveniently decried a headache, leaving us to ourselves. I'd been waiting all day to hear what was to become of me.

He tented his fingers. "I cannot fathom why anyone would deceive Lord Camden in such a way. I'm not certain what to think."

"Do you believe he tells the truth?" I doubted his words.

"I do not know." He brushed biscuit crumbs from his jacket, lowering his voice. "Lord Sherborne has not replied to my query."

I sipped my tea, throat tight.

"The bad part about living near a small village is that everyone knows everyone else's business. Even if I relocated you to the good vicar's home, everyone would know it by nightfall. And I wouldn't be there to protect you."

"What could Lord Sherborne do for me?"

"He is another matter entirely. I had hoped he would see you safely escorted away. Unseen." He looked to the nearby servant and back to me again. "I've talked with Simpson. He says he was shaken awake by the housekeeper and told of your illness. Rothy says she got this knowledge from a maid of yours, who denies saying any such thing. The other servant is nowhere to be found."

I started, spilling my tea. "Gone, like Mary?"

"Yes."

"So when Lord Camden saw that I wasn't in my bed…"

"He panicked apparently. He hopes the maids have run off rather than deal with another death on his property. An investigation would taint Camden's reputation. Which he needs if he's going to come through on the Banbury case."

"Banbury." Of whose scandals I was entirely ignorant. "The man that died last week uttered the name with his last breath."

"Yes. I imagine there's hardly a soul in England who hasn't heard of his devious escapades. Thanks to Lord Sherborne's work, much of the man's wicked deeds have become public."

"What did Banbury do?" I wasn't sure I wanted to know.

"The worst things possible. Lady Sherborne's family's shipping company was destroyed by his games. As well as the local Chinworth family—Mr. Chinworth confessed to his dealings with the man. Lord Camden dabbled here and there—not fully knowing the dishonorable nature of his speculating..."

"The letter of denial that he signed? About his dealings with Banbury?"

"Yes. Quite."

"But the dead man seemed to know Lord Camden. Spoke directly to him."

"That worries me. Greatly. But what can I do? I merely represent the family in the inheritance case and—his unfortunate dealings. He hopes the issue will pass without difficulty."

"Do you think it will?"

Ewan shook his head. "No. I do not." He swallowed more tea. "I didn't tell you, but the past few mornings when I've left your hall, I've spotted Lord Camden returning to the house with a shovel—rather muddied. He has moved about as though he doesn't want to be seen."

"He's looking for what the dead man buried, isn't he?"

"I believe so."

"Must be quite a fortune."

"Fortune? Or, Jane, what if the dead man buried evidence that would point directly to him?" Ewan shook his head. "His involvement with Banbury may be far greater than I imagined."

Two maids had disappeared. And a horse. I'd been attacked. My clothing destroyed. Dr. Rillian had given us weapons from Sherborne. There was so much more to this than what we could see. If only I could understand what I had to do with any of it—aside from Ewan's findings.

"I truly cannot tell if he knows what I've found in the family documents. Last night, I was so certain. Now?" He shook his head. "I simply don't know."

A maid entered and dipped a curtsy. "Lady Camden would see you, Miss. In her private room."

I rose and followed her, feeling Ewan's gaze at my back...

She guided me through the newer part of Butterton Hall, Down a single, wide corridor not nearly as ancient as the wing where I'd been placed, and opened a door to an opulent room.

"Lady Camden, I trust you are well?"

"My head, dear. Poor me. It spins when I move." A smallish turban wound over her frayed white hair, her wig of dark curls rested on a nearby table. She waved me closer. "You are looking in the pink of health, my dear." She smiled, showing all of her teeth.

"I thank you."

"Send for Doctor Rillian and have the stitches removed."

"He comes this night, Lady Camden."

She clapped her jeweled hands together. "Perfect timing. I did tell you that a bevy of gentlemen comes your way soon, didn't I? Lord Camden's annual winter fox hunt?"

She had not told me, but I would play along. "A fox hunt, is it?" I very much doubted I'd be here for the event. Not that I even wanted to participate under such strange circumstances.

"Come now, I must have mentioned it. Hmm. A riding habit is being delivered on the morrow for you. Bright red. Will suit your coloring I should think." Her face grew serious. "Our guests arrive the day after tomorrow—more than a few single gentlemen among them." She winked.

Her intentions were ever so clear. Twas no fox hunt, but a husband hunt. Only I was the hunted. Would that Mr. Stevens saw me far from here before this event occurred.

Lady Camden pursed her lips. "I will be hiring extra servant girls from the village since Mary and that other one abandoned us."

She couldn't even remember her name! It seemed she'd left the Hogmanay curse at the conclusion of Twelfth Night. I only hoped the maid had fled and no other ill befell them. I left after Lady Camden had finished her unending plans for the house party. She'd taken care to hand me a list outlining exactly, in excruciating detail, what I must wear each day.

Never mind my tastes, my desires. I wished for my old clothing, my old life. The old me. But I had outgrown any thought of actually living like the Camdens—yet the life before me seemed too large. Where and how did I fit within it?

After supper, I sat in the library while Dr. Rillian removed the stitches. He spoke quietly while Ewan leaned in.

"Lord Sherborne requests that you both stay here for the time being. It is imperative." He slipped a thread away from my skin with tweezers. "There is more at stake than you realize. Much more."

I pressed a hand to my heart to slow the rapid beating. If only it would. "What do I have to do with these so-called stakes?"

"Maybe nothing, Miss Hartford. Yet all must appear to be in order, then he will make his mistake…"

"What mistake exactly will that be?" I wondered who might be harmed next.

"Time will tell." He made a final snip and tug. "Sherborne's sending two men over to work as servants. They will look out for you both. And keep a wary eye on any use of his shovel."

Ewan's lips grew taught. "I cannot allow another risk on Jane's life."

Dr. Rillian smiled. "Jane, is it?" He winked. "Well then, stay close to her. Very close. The Banbury case should distract Lord Camden for a while. The man doesn't want scandals attached to his name. His vanity and need for a clean reputation will keep you safe, for now, Miss Hartford, if he is your attacker, that is."

If only I could believe that.

Ewan grasped Dr. Rillian's hand and shook it. "Thank you, doctor. The men attending the fox hunt are well-known about the Ton. Their visit buys us time and some measure of protection, at any rate."

"You will be joining them, I hope?"

Ewan nodded. "The invitation has been graciously extended my direction."

"Very good. Might prove useful."

I hoped the doctor was right.

Chapter Nine

Growing up, I'd only been a bystander, watching fox hunts from a distance. Though Chilham Castle sent invitations to Father and Sir Jones, they never took part.

Now, I stood as one of the party amid the throng of experienced hunters, feeling rather resplendent in my red riding habit, but also feeling quite the fraud since I'd never before ridden a horse. A detail Lady Camden failed to ask—and that I didn't think to offer.

The event had started the night before in a dizzying flurry of light snow. Carriage after carriage pulled up to Butterton Hall, bearing gentlemen, a few women, and a bevy of servants. By the next morning, the hall was a buzzing hive.

I'd been introduced to all of them and much to my chagrin, this poor vicar's daughter failed to remember virtually every name. I breakfasted for the first time downstairs. Not a single distinguished gentleman regarded me even briefly or spoke a word to me save a grunted greeting. I didn't mind, though it did not bode well for matchmaking success.

Mr. Stevens came to my side, an encouraging smile on his lips. "You look well in red."

"I thank you.

"I hope you enjoy the afternoon, despite..."

"Yes." Despite the fearful unknown.

I wouldn't be riding with the gentlemen down the lane like some of the younger ladies. Rather, I would see them off from the stables and find a quiet corner to rest. Ewan wasn't able to guard my door from the outside last night as he'd been doing. Too many guests had been placed in rooms along the usually empty hall. The risk of his being seen was too great. I'd shoved my trunk against the door and kept my dagger close. Surely the presence of the company would keep danger at bay.

I made my way outside with the rest of the party when Lord Camden drew me to his side. "Come along with me, child." A rare smile formed about his lips. "I have something for you." His smile grew tight, his eyes strained.

A burly, unsmiling man—the gamekeeper, I assumed—brought forward a horse. "A gift for my cousin!"

Such a shock! To gift me with this... beast? Surely, he didn't expect me to ride? I wore a riding habit. Of course, he expected it.

The guests applauded. This couldn't be happening.

Someone shouted, "Well done, Camden. She's a beaut."

The gamekeeper clicked his teeth, then spat onto the frozen ground before handing me the reigns.

I had hoped to go entirely unnoticed, but now, every eye was upon me.

One of the gentlemen patted the beast's thigh. "Right smart one, she is."

The horse's head nickered high above mine. "Thank you, Lord Camden...I..." Perhaps he *was* trying to murder me.

He gave a short nod and entirely ignored me as he made his way to his steed, making no offer to assist.

Everyone began mounting their horses.

"See here, she's fitted perfectly for you, Miss Hartford." A stable hand placed a mounting block beside her.

Dread swept through me. The animal was huge. I wouldn't be able to properly mount.

"Here, let me help." Ewan approached.

"By all means."

The stable hand took the reins as Ewan began to instruct. "Your right knee will go here." He patted the saddle. "And your left leg should be here." He smiled. "Ready?"

"Now or never."

"Give me your left foot. That's it, now—"

I landed on the saddle with ease.

He placed my foot in the stirrup. "Keep your boot firmly placed and your knee straight. That's right. Comfortable?"

I couldn't answer. How thankful I was for his kindness.

The stable boy slipped a cane into my hands. "Hold steady, miss."

Ewan spoke to the boy holding my horse. "Stay with her, I'll be right back."

He mounted his own steed and rode to my side. "Take the reins but do not pull them."

"Must I do this?" Fear arched within.

He smiled stiffly. "Lord Camden made a gift to you before the party. I think it best, for a few paces at least."

I nodded.

"I will stay with you."

His assurance quelled my nerves a little. With fanfare and much barking, the gamekeeper brought the hounds out while the horses stamped in place, anticipating the run—but I dared not be distracted from my attempt to stay atop the beast.

Did Lord Camden seek my death by horse-riding accident? The animal swayed beneath me as she moved ahead.

"Hold the pommel with your left hand if you must. That's it. Use your cane just so. See? What did I tell you? No one notices those of us at the end of the queue. We can go at our ease. When Lord Camden and the rest of the party head off, I will help you down and we'll walk back together. Easy enough."

I swallowed back fear and let myself look up. Two other ladies were upon their horses. They intended to join the hunt—I heard them say as much at breakfast.

"You look a portrait." He smiled.

I didn't recognize myself in the mirror this morning. Covered in trailing bright red fabric, the cut was rather becoming and the jet-black buttons were indeed dazzling. Yet the face beneath the matching feathered hat didn't belong in such glittering garb. "It is a sin to tell a lie, Mr. Stevens."

"I am always honest. To a fault, some say."

This I believed. He would pursue the strange documents linking my family line to Butterton Hall. The truth will set you free, as Father used to quote. That verse spoke of the truth of His word, of following Truth. Christ Himself.

At that moment I understood. He had guided me here. Was no mistake. I was meant to be here, to experience the curiosities, the difficulties. Perhaps even to meet Mr. Ewan Stevens. But would the truth – and mysteries – of Butterton Hall set anyone free?

We followed the party farther down the lane until several of the hounds bayed. Their howls set the horses to a run. They were off—and away from us.

The gamekeeper glanced back at me with a hard stare before following the group. I didn't wonder. One such as I didn't belong on so fine a beast. Several stable boys followed on smaller ponies. Ewan and I were left alone. Quite alone. Not that I minded.

"There now. You can relax, Jane."

I took a deep breath. "Might I get down? Please."

"Certainly." He disembarked and while holding the reins of his horse, helped me down, his arms about me tightened to keep me from falling. How long had it been since I'd been held so close? Not since Father passed. But Ewan Stevens wasn't Father.

He held me for a moment, his eyes a gentle stroke upon my face, my name a whisper on his lips, "Jane." I sensed his regard—his care. My heart became unsteady, my breathing shallow. Did he care? Like that? Oh, how I hoped.

He removed his arm from my back and took the reins of both horses. "You did splendidly. If only you'd landed in a happier place, I should have had great pleasure in teaching you to ride."

"I should have liked that." Butterton Hall was not a happy place. "What am I to do when the party leaves?"

"I await Lord Sherborne's instructions."

"Is he to be obeyed?" Truly trusted?

"Yes. He is. He is a man you can trust with your life. One who would sacrifice his own for the greater good if it came to that."

"He is like you, I think."

"Like me? How so?"

"I believe you to be the same sort of man." Was true. He'd been not only kind but a protective shield for me. Close and caring.

He turned his head in denial. "You give me too high a praise." He craned his neck to look past my shoulder. "Someone comes, and at great speed. The lad will break his neck if he isn't careful."

I turned. A young messenger on horseback sped down the road and stopped before Mr. Stevens, hatless and out of breath. "It's Chinworth, sir. Mr. Chinworth of Mayfield Manor! He's been murdered!"

"How do you mean? Calm yourself, lad."

"The old man, Mr. Chinworth. He were killed in his cell, weren't he?" He took a deep breath. "The magistrate sent me to tell ye—and to tell Lord Camden directly."

Ewan's jaw grew taught. "I'll see it done."

The messenger rode away.

"He'll be off to see Lord Sherborne next, I'll wager."

A boy rushed from the stables at our approach. "Here, take Miss Hartford's horse. I must find Lord Camden with all haste."

He squeezed my hand. "I will explain later."

I watched Ewan race back the way we came, urgency in every gallop. Mr. Chinworth had been murdered. I'd heard the name a few times. Ewan had been frustrated that Lord Camden had dined with a Tobias Chinworth the night of my arrival. Was Tobias his son? And again, when he told me of some of the Banbury scandal, that the elder Mr. Chinworth was somehow connected to some crimes.

One man had already died with the Banbury name on his lips. The desperate Hogmanay stranger. How did these deaths affect Lord Camden? And by way of approximation, me?

I was alone. Vulnerable. If Lord Camden was innocent, then I was a wide-open target for anyone else. If I only knew why this was happening... I felt for my dagger, carefully hidden, strapped to my leg.

I made my way back up the steps and through the grand foyer. The ladies that remained behind sat in the grand drawing room, laughter flowing as easily as tea from the pot. Lady Camden filled the doorway.

"You've returned already! Excellent. Now we may set your course once and for all." She turned to the guests with a dramatic sweep of her bejeweled hand. "Tell us ladies, which gentleman would suit my beautiful cousin?"

More laughter ensued and handkerchiefs fluttered. I began to question whether I was wise to leave the perch on my horse.

A man had just died. Why did I feel like this tragedy had everything to do with me? The thought nagged and worried.

For the space of an hour, the older ladies patted my hands, turned me about like a roll of linen, and affixed my fate to some gentleman or another. I was sure to catch someone's eye, they said. How encouraging. In fact, alas, it seemed I already had.

"Mr. Rushforth should do for her very well. Small estate, but quite fine. She'll want for nothing."

"Why no, my dear. He is far too plump."

More giggles and laughter and tea. Until the men came tearing back to the front of the house. Far earlier than expected. Horses reared up with forelegs churning high. Shouts could be heard. Ewan had delivered the news—news that created quite a stir.

Lady Camden stood. "Dear me, what is that uproar? What is happening?" She stamped her foot at the shouting, the noise. "This is outrageous"

I wondered if she would begin shrieking.

The dogs whined amid angry voices. Disappointment overwhelmed all. The dogs were deprived of the catch, the horses a good run, and the men the sport of finding a terrified fox. Why did the death of a criminal, though a gentleman, create such a fury?

Lady Camden squinted her eyes and peered through the window. "Lord Camden seems ill." She fanned herself. "Simpson? Simpson!" Her voice boomed.

Lord Camden crumpled to the ground as Lady Camden ran from the room and down the few steps to his side. Should I have followed? I stayed in place, hardly knowing the impact of the news. Obviously, Mr. Chinworth was a significant figure. His death, a reason to halt all activity.

One of the ladies joined me at the window. "I do hope Lord Camden isn't ill."

I cleared my throat. "I suppose he has weakened from the shock." Though I didn't know why.

"The shock of what, speak plain, my dear. Don't mumble."

"A Mr. Chinworth, it is reported, has been murdered."

A short gasp met my ears.

Lady Camden lifted her face and shouted to a servant. "Send for Dr. Rillian!" Then, released one high shriek, and fainted. One by one, the women left, some joined their husbands, and others retired to their rooms.

The ruckus eventually died down but I sensed fear as thick as fog. Nearly every man appeared uncomfortable. But an odd few seemed only perturbed at their sport being interrupted.

Ewan strode to my side, brows raised. "That was one way to separate the sheep from the goats."

I thought of the Bible verse. "How do you mean?"

"Most of the men have had dealings with Banbury in some fashion. Or Chinworth for that matter." He snatched a biscuit from a forgotten plate on the tea table and chewed absently. "The Camden's seem especially grieved."

"Both of them swooned." An outrageous show.

"I understand the sadness of a loss, he was a neighbor after all." He ate another biscuit. "But not to this degree. One does not swoon for mere neighbors."

"No. Not often." I had not fainted at my Father's passing. I wept for days, yes. But nothing more.

I peered from the window again. A carriage pulled around the side of the original entrance. "Look—some of the guests are leaving."

He glanced around me, the warmth of his face close to mine. "Hmm. I am not at all surprised."

I swallowed as the heat became a blaze about my face. "Why such haste?"

"I believe it is hard to fire at moving targets."

"Target?" The word snapped my mind to attention. I faced him.

"Mr. Chinworth isn't the only murder of someone connected to Banbury." He moved away, pulling back the curtain and looking farther down the path. The cool air chased away the heat. "Someone is out there, picking off anyone grossly tied to the man. Self-appointed justice, it seems."

My hand went to my throat. "The man that died in the drawing room...on New Year's..."

"His wounds were no accident. Someone meant to kill him, and succeeded."

But I was not connected to Banbury. Not in any way whatsoever.

One of the servants approached with a message on a silver tray for Ewan. I guessed it to be from one of Lord Sherborne's men.

Ewan read it quickly and nodded. "I will return this evening for dinner. Do stay near other people, won't you?" He bowed and left me.

I retreated to my room to pray. What else could I do? Indeed, Father had often said it to be the most important action.

Chapter Ten

I changed from my riding habit into a more practical gown, if any of Lady Camden's unique choices might be called such. I checked the place where I'd hidden the twenty pounds. Still there. Good. Might I need to carry this gift on my person at all times? I tucked it into my half boots.

Would I have to flee Butterton Hall? And, if so, when? Luncheon was announced, but only a few made their way to the dining hall—and no one was in a conversant mood.

The palpable fear I'd sensed earlier had combined with a taut strain. One gentleman's hand trembled as he reached for a mug of mulled cider. His eyes darted. He swallowed his food nearly whole. I'd seen these strange actions before when Father and I visited a thief who planned to confess that very hour. Was this fellow guilty too? In some way connected to Banbury's evil schemes?

The guilty very often crumble from within. We aren't meant to do evil, and it kills us if we do. At least for those with a conscience.

Confession and repentance—those elements that set Christianity apart from all other beliefs—can bring about redemption if we believe in the One who cast his own body to the judgment we all deserve. If the man believed that he was knit by the hands of God and loved, truly loved, his hand wouldn't want to touch evil. Not after truly knowing that kind of love.

I wanted to tell him to run to Christ. And quickly. As it was, I sat too far across the table. He took a final swallow of his cider and sped from the room.

Wherever the man goes, Lord, I pray he soon finds You and reaches for You.

I began to pray more. For each person yet residing in this place. For Butterton's protection. For Ewan and whatever part Lord Sherborne played in the Banbury scandal.

I left the luncheon table and returned to my room.

Oh no! Someone had been here again. This time, my things were overturned and scattered about. But at least they weren't shredded.

A middle-aged footman stalled in my doorway, his dark eyes blinked in concern. "Miss Hartford? Are you alright?"

One of Lord Sherborne's men? I hoped so.

"I'm fine, as you can see. However, my things are not." My journal. The pages I'd written on had been ripped out, stolen.

He lowered his voice. "Do record anything of note that you find missing. No matter how seemingly insignificant. When you've finished, meet me down the old stairs. No one is using them—most of the servants have gone with the guests by now."

I nodded, looking around the room with greater attention.

"I won't be far." He bowed and left.

Lord Sherborne was wrong. The Banbury scandal wasn't keeping my enemy at bay. Whoever he may be. At this point, I couldn't believe it to be Lord Camden. Not after seeing him buckle to the ground earlier. Hopefully, Dr. Rillian had been attending the Camdens after the shock and could attest to his not leaving his room while recovering.

My mind spun as I gazed upon the mess. My clothing, at least, was intact. My personal things remained—things no one should have a care to look upon—my memories, some of my father's sermons. Old letters I hadn't wanted to part with from parishioners whom we'd dearly loved—they were, unfortunately, violated. Scattered about, trampled upon. As though someone intended to hurt my heart.

I allowed myself a good cry before making the list. That's when I noticed something of significance was indeed missing. Father's Bible. I searched everywhere hoping it might have been tossed beneath the bed or thrown into the wardrobe. But no. The worn treasure had been taken. Possibly lost to me forever.

For a thief to take such a thing bewildered me. I quickly gathered my list and retreated down the old stairs. The man was waiting.

"The most important item missing is my father's Bible. Other than that, pages from my journal, though I'm sure it made for some boring reading..." I shrugged. "Most of my things were either dumped out or trampled upon. Very little was taken."

"He took the foolscap from my hands. "Thank you, Miss Hartford. I'll make sure that Lord Sherborne is apprised of these developments." He bowed. "Might I suggest taking refuge in the library today?" He winked. "A good book can make light of a heavy day, I find."

I nodded. He wanted me to stay in the library where I might be kept safe. Good idea.

"Straightaway, then." His glance dictated that he be obeyed. Very well.

Nerves constricted my mid-section. As I made my way to the cozy, book-filled room, all I could think about was the dagger strapped to my leg and the twenty pounds I'd slipped into my shoe.

It was but two o'clock in the afternoon. Ewan wouldn't return until supper. Then, would I finally know how to proceed? I slipped into the blessedly empty room.

Perhaps some poems or a novel would keep my mind occupied. I hoped, at least, for that outcome. I settled into a chair by the fire—one that faced the open doorway—with a book of poetry in my hands. Appropriate for a stressful afternoon.

I tried to focus on the words, but couldn't. A very idle hour later, tea was brought to me. I spent the better part of the next hour perusing the many volumes and finally resettled with a large book filled with ink drawings of English villages. Interesting in a very dull way. I yawned and grew drowsy.

A grandfather clock's bells chimed six times. I jerked from my chair. When had I fallen asleep? The book I'd been perusing had tumbled from my lap.

A soft chuckle sounded from beside me and I startled. "Seemed a shame to wake you."

"Ewan!" My face grew hot. "I mean, Mr. Stevens. Forgive me."

"Please," he reached out his hand. "I'd like you to use my Christian name."

"Very well. When we are alone, at least." I offered a smile. "Most of the party has fled."

"So I noticed." He set the volume I'd been reading on the table between us. "I'm not at all surprised."

"And Lord Sherborne?"

"Is rather put out." Ewan bit his lower lip and rubbed the day's growth on his jaw. "Dr. Rillian is here attending the Camdens. Did you know?"

"I hoped." I drew my shawl about my shoulders as the room had grown colder with the night. "Were you told what happened in my room? To my things?"

He solemnly nodded. "I hesitate to tell you, but that was quite unforeseen."

"Has Lord Camden been informed?"

He shook his head. "He has been under the influence of laudanum since collapsing this morning."

"I don't understand. We both saw him in my room!"

"Which he explained, Jane. Even the maid and the butler corroborate his story."

"Perhaps Lady Camden is the one who is mad."

Ewan took a deep breath. "I have been here for a few months and she may be many things, but she is not mad. Angry, to be sure, but she does not suffer from insanity. Besides, she's been asleep these several hours."

I conceded. An accusation like that would send her to an asylum where patients entered but few returned home. I ought to be careful, and yet... "My clothing...the first time..."

"Perhaps a form of madness does reside here—but I would think such strangeness would strike randomly—and not just—" he swallowed and looked me in the eye, "you."

As the party had entirely vacated Butterton Hall, and Lord and Lady Camden were indisposed, supper was brought to us in the library, to the table by the window where I had first dined.

A rich spread lay before us— the food had no doubt been intended to impress the guests and needed to be used. We willingly ate. For all the unpleasant events and questions that arose from them, the hot meal did much to bolster my spirit. Indeed, the feast rivaled Christmas, New Years, and Twelfth Night with a variety of meats and gravy, fruit compotes, tender potatoes, and hot rolls.

"I do believe now would be a good time to show you the letter from your great-grandfather—and the information I found." He rose and pulled my chair. "My study isn't far." He picked up a chamber stick and lit the wick at the fire in the hearth. "Come." He held out his hand.

When we exited the library, I noted the footman from earlier, following us. With my life seemingly at stake, propriety had to be set aside.

Ewan lit a few more candles and opened a desk drawer. He rifled through some parchments. Then, checked another drawer. Even in the dim light, I could see his face pale. "It's gone." He combed his fingers through his hair and stood. "I've told no one, Jane, except for Lord Sherborne." He came to my side and took my hand. "I am sorry. I don't know what to do. That letter was a significant piece of evidence—"

"Stop." I held my hand up. "This estate—I do not expect to claim it. Nor do I want it."

He nodded. "I understand. His fingers tightened around mine. "But you need to understand that someone sees you as a threat. The entire file concerning the ownership of this estate isn't here. It's been stolen. And someone knows the truth."

Someone? Lord or Lady Camden? "My father's Bible was taken from my room…"

"Bibles often contain a family record of births and marriages."

It made sense now. "So," I swallowed, "this isn't about Banbury…but…"

"Your heritage."

"Oh." My mouth went try. I was a threat. There was a record in the Bible, one that began with my great, great grandfather…

"If anything, those papers would have provided a motive to the courts."

"A motive for…"

His eyes flashed. "You've been gravely assaulted, Jane." He placed his hands on my shoulders. "I would see justice served." He looked down, both tenderness and strength in his eyes.

I trembled. "But at what cost?"

His hand came under my jaw. "Your life is in danger now, and the fact that your great-grandfather faked his death isn't public knowledge. If I don't pursue this, the cost, Jane, might be too high."

My life would be the cost. And the Banbury scandal? The perfect distraction from anyone taking close notice of a poor vicar's daughter. Would that I had stayed in Chilham. Where I was safe.

"I must leave."

"Indeed."

"When?"

"We cannot leave tonight. The household would notice something amiss. No, we shall leave on the morrow. Lady Sherborne has invited you to tea. I will escort you there. All will appear in order—you will feign an illness and won't be able to return. It is the only way they can safely house you."

I agreed to the plan. "Lady Sherborne is very kind."

"She is kindness itself."

"Let us tarry in the library before retiring." He blew out the candles. "I do not want you to sleep in your room tonight. Not after what happened."

"A long night in the library seems my only option."

"No. You'll be staying with me, in my room."

Scandalous... yet, he'd stayed with me the night Lord Camden had entered my room. Logic bid that such oversight was not indecent. Indecent would be if he'd left me vulnerable. But if we were discovered, the ramifications would either leave my future in shambles or he would be forced to wed me. My mouth grew dry at both prospects.

His eyes sought mine. "Jane. I know what I ask. And I know what I mean to do." His hands took mine. "We cannot spend this much time together and maintain respectability."

I understood. "We must soon part ways." The obvious answer.

He shook his head. "You would not be safe." He continued, "At Lord Sherborne's urging, I've purchased a common license."

My breath caught. I repeated his words, "A common license?" He spoke of a union. Of marriage.

"It is only fair." He pushed a hand through his hair again. "I'm the one who brought you here into this dark lair. I take full responsibility for your safety."

My face burned. "I would not force you to suffer the consequence of an unwanted marriage."

"Suffer?" Amusement bent around his lips. He bent to my ear. "I assure you, being married to you would be no trial."

"We haven't known each other but a few weeks, and yet—" I stumbled through the tangled vines of my thoughts and feelings.

He finished my sentence. "And yet I feel as though we've known each other forever. I've never met a better woman." His voice grew serious and quiet. "Nor do I wish to meet another. You're all I have ever hoped for."

He need not feel bound by duty, however much my heart would burst at the thought of being loved by one such as he. "This poor mouse of a vicar's daughter—" I looked up hesitantly.

"Is a diamond. Miss Jane Hartford, will you consent to be my wife that I may offer you not only my protection but my unfailing love?"

I stalled, the beauty, the grace of the moment stole my breath. He wanted to marry me. And not just for propriety's sake. Delight overwhelmed me. Still, I found no words to respond.

He didn't wait for a reply but captured my mouth with his. Sweetness, far sweeter than honey. His gentle caress swayed my heart into believing that I could well spend the rest of my life with Ewan Stevens.

He leaned his head against mine. "I do hope you will say yes."

I smiled. "How could I not?"

"I'm still waiting for an answer."

"Yes, Mr. Stevens. I will marry you."

Relief spread across his face as he kissed my warm cheek. "We have plans to make. We will be able to marry in two days."

"Two days..." So quick...

He slipped a ring from his pinky and onto my hand. "My family's signet. Wear it until I can provide another. It is my pledge to you."

I nodded waiting for what would come next.

Chapter Eleven

Hours later, well after midnight, he secreted me within his room. Exhaustion flooded my body. How had so much happened in one, singular day? I swayed, nearly toppling off my feet.

"You are overly tired." Ewan lifted me, settled me on the bed, and drew a blanket to my shoulders. "Sleep, if you can. I will keep watch." He sat across the room, his dagger within reach.

Regardless of our intent to marry, being in his room without a third party grated against my sensibilities and my very proper upbringing. But there was no other way. We would marry. Yes. This I knew I must do. I stroked the impression on the ring—a cross swords with a cluster of primroses atop. Love and protection...my eyes were so very heavy...

An hour later, I jerked awake. Dr. Rillian had come—he and Ewan were speaking in low, tense tones. I sat up, straining to hear.

Ewan rushed to my side. "My dear. Another attempt on your life has been made."

I clutched the bedpost. "I am safe, as you see."

He shook his head. "Your room was set to rights and then made to look as though you slept beneath the covers." He pulled a knife from beneath his coat. A kitchen knife. "I thank God that naught but goose down pillows were destroyed."

"You mean to say..." A fiery heat spread across my chest, stoking fear.

Ewan's face grew hard. "Someone tried to kill you, and not by accident this time."

This time... How many more attempts would there be?

Dr. Rillian continued, "Sherborne's men saw two figures enter the room."

"Lord Camden one of them?"

"I cannot say since I was dismissed to my room hours ago." His mouth drew a grim line. "You must take Miss Hartford from Butterton Hall as soon as may be."

"I agree." Ewan grabbed his coat and some personal effects.

"Ride to Sherborne. Nothing for it, man." Dr. Rillian turned to me. "Don't concern yourself about your belongings. We'll see them returned to you as soon as possible."

My belongings? A few trinkets from childhood. The few old letters, now trampled and torn. Some well-read books. A pennywhistle. My ripped journal. In truth, I owned nothing of consequence, except... I touched the signet ring again—I would soon own a new name.

A shriek sounded and I jolted. Lady Camden? She screamed again. "Oh no."

Dr. Rillian rolled his eyes. "Lady Camden rises from the dead to scream like a raging banshee. Right, then."

The shrieks continued, as did footsteps pounding up and down the hall.

Ewan pursed his lips. "There will be no escape for us this night."

Dr. Rillian shook his head. "You must." He looked to the door. "They'll be sending for me, I shouldn't wonder, but do wait until I return." He pointed a finger at Ewan. "Might you be off soon to pay a visit to the anvil-priest? Or have the banns read, like a decent chap? Do the right thing, Stevens." He smiled.

Ewan bowed. "As we have recently planned, but not in Gretna Green."

A light flicked in his eye. "Good. I shan't be long."

I looked from the window. A lantern floated in the night, the figure carrying it too shadowed to see. Would that Butterton Hall and the murderous plot that stalked me were already far behind us.

Ewan's hands cupped my shoulders. "Soon, we will take our leave."

Another shriek rent the air. One shrill moan after the other. Sobbing filled the hall, as footsteps slowed. Ewan motioned to me to stay hidden behind the door as he opened it and inquired.

"What has happened?"

A maid's voice trembled. "The housekeeper, sir, she be dead!"

Coils of cold snaked around my middle.

"How did it come to be?" Ewan asked.

"No one knows, sir. She was taking chocolate to Lady Camden and fell over, she did! Chocolate and all! Quite a mess."

"You mean she collapsed?"

"Far as I know."

"Thank you."

"Sir."

Ewan shut the door and bolted it. "We must pray, Jane." He took my hand and bowed, silent and still.

Sometime later, Dr. Rillian returned to us. "The woman is not dead, but nearly so. Whatever has happened, her heart is weak, whether by nature or by shock, I do not know. She is resting as comfortably as I can make her."

Ewan released my hand. "No sign of foul play?"

"None that the eye can see." He buttoned his jacket. "She is such a grim creature, one can only wonder. Lady Camden has summoned the vicar. She is concerned that the Hogmanay curse is still upon this place."

The tall, blond gentleman had stepped through Butterton Hall's door within the first five minutes of the New Year and promptly died. But no, our troubles did not begin there. My ruined gowns testified to that fact. Twas an older curse at work. Greed.

Dr. Rillian shook Ewan's hand. "Hastings will guard you. He is at the ready now. Do ride safely."

Ewan nodded his thanks.

"Here, put this on." His cloak. He strapped a small satchel around his shoulder and cracked open the door. "All clear." He held a finger to his lips before taking my hand.

We walked in the dark shadows of the Hall and made our way to the stable easily enough. The staff that remained awake must have been busy tending the Camdens and the poor housekeeper.

"I must saddle my horse," he whispered. "Kneel behind this barrel."

I did as told. Ewan was gone for several long minutes before returning.

He lifted me onto the large beast and climbed behind me. He held the reins with his right hand, but his left wrapped tightly around me.

A half-moon guided us. I wondered at the man who was to be my husband. I had been told that unless men entered the ministry, they wouldn't be particularly religious until knocking at death's door. That men of every sort only tolerated church as a means to appease their wives and mothers. For certain, I'd seen such charade at play, and even now, churches are largely filled with women-folk. But Ewan had begged us to pray. And he meant it.

We rode slowly in the shadows. He guided the horse along wooded areas, away from the road. He leaned in and whispered in my ear. "Someone follows us. I do hope it's only Hastings."

His grip around my waist tightened.

Shuffling and light snaps filtered through the trees.

"They are too close," he whispered.

I shuddered from both cold and fear.

"We must run for the woods." In an instant, he was off the horse and pulled me down after him. He grabbed my hand and we ran, the moon hidden behind clouds, so I could scarcely see.

A loud crack and flash of fire lit the air.

Ewan made a turn and another. Minutes later, we heard another shot in the distance. We panted heavily, indeed, my lungs hurt, I could scarcely draw breath. We collapsed at the base of a large tree.

"We are lost. I am not familiar with these woods." He pulled me close to his side and wrapped an arm around my shoulder. "We'll have to wait here until daybreak."

"What if they find us?" Darkness, his face was a shadow.

"They won't." He took my free hand. "We must be still and quiet."

The sound of our panting may give us away. I was too loud. "I can't stop." The panic of the moment ran amuck in my mind. Someone tried to kill me again.

"Breathe deep and slow. That's it. I will keep you safe." After some time, I was finally able to draw a normal breath. He drew my head to his chest and whispered, "Try to get some sleep."

His heartbeat quickened, then slowed, and I with that strong rhythm in my ear, slept.

I jolted awake at the sound of a click and a shotgun bayonet pointed at us. We'd been discovered.

Ewan's grip tightened. "Put that down, man, before you hurt someone."

The owner of the weapon stood tall with ruddy long hair and a well-kept beard. He spat to the side. "And why should I do that?"

Ewan shifted, the man flinched.

"Because we are innocents lost in a wood. All we want is to get out of it and eat a hearty breakfast." Sarcasm laced his voice.

The man jerked his head. "You married?"

My skin burned with panic.

"Soon to be, as a matter of fact."

"You steal her away from her father, is that it? He didn't agree to the marriage? Sounds like poachin' to me."

"I am most certainly not poaching."

He shrugged. "Takin' what doesn't belong to you…"

I had to speak up. "You must be the gamekeeper." I swallowed at the hard lump in my throat. "I am of age and of free will. This man hasn't taken anything—or anyone."

The man only grinned.

"Hoskins, do let Mr. Stevens and Miss Hartford alone." Lord Sherborne appeared wearing old clothing and an equally vintage tri-corn hat. "Not exactly time for a jest, man."

"Sorry, my lord. Didn't mean no harm." Hoskins lowered his weapon.

Lord Sherborne lifted his hat and replaced it. "I've been searching for you for hours. When Dr. Rillian sent word that you'd be arriving soon, and then you didn't—" he spread his hands open, "well, here you are. Safe and sound. Thank God."

Ewan stood and drew me to my feet, relief flooding my nerves. "We were shot at—had to make a run for it. Surely your man, Hoskins here, didn't think we were…" he coughed, "poaching?"

"Wasn't Hoskins, he's been with me the night through. But that is bad news." He flicked his eyes to the tall, gun-wielding man. "You know what to do."

He nodded, bowed deeply to me, "Miss Hartford, do forgive me. I didn't know." He clicked his teeth. "Find all manner of doings in these woods." With a nod to Ewan, he left.

Lord Sherborne smiled. "Do come have breakfast." He led the way. "I believe there is a wedding to take place soon?"

I blinked in the pale sunlight filtering through the trees. A wedding. Mine...

"Oh, and we found your horse, Stevens. Callum brushed the poor, frightened beast and gave him a sack of oats."

"I must thank him."

As we made our way to Goodwyn Abbey, I felt each and every muscle burn. My frozen feet didn't want to work.

"Right then." Ewan swooshed me into his arms and carried me close until we reached the estate.

The atmosphere felt so different there. As soon as we stepped through the door, I sensed peace. Joy. Hope. All the elements had been missing from Butterton Hall. Attributes I hadn't sensed since leaving Sir and Lady Jones and the rickety iron gates of Glen Park. Homesickness pure and simple.

Mrs. Jones had said that it was time to dream in other places, to live a new adventure. Though I'd had to live a nightmare, hope had never seemed too far away. I knew God was with me, whatever I encountered.

And there was Ewan. I glanced at his unshaven jaw and the concerned wrinkles around his eyes. He cared for me. I believed that. And I cared for him. Deeply. Miraculous in such little time we'd known each other—and yet I felt as though I'd always known him.

A gift from God amid winter's darkness. Help had never been far. Regardless of the fear that whoever sought to end my life would succeed, these gifts seemed stronger. More capable. Powerful.

We entered the house by the back way where I was ushered immediately to a small, warm room. Lady Sherborne awaited us.

"Dear Jane!" She opened her arm. "Come. I've had a hot bath drawn for you."

I couldn't control the tears that dripped down my face. "I assure you I am more than thankful. And relieved."

She nodded. "I believe I heard that you are to be a bride come tomorrow morning."

"It is rather sudden." Did she approve?

"I understand more than you know." She lifted the cloak from my shoulders as I shuddered before the snapping fire. "Have you heard the story of how Lord Sherborne and I met and married?"

"I have not."

"There," she pointed, "Behind the screen you'll find the bath. And while you soak, I will tell you everything."

I sat in the warmth for a long while, listening to every detail. I confess to being very surprised.

"I daresay you'll find much in common with dear Emma and Joseph too. They will arrive by nightfall." She slipped a stack of towels onto a chair near the tub. "The Carters are related to the recently deceased Mr. Chinworth."

"I wish I understood. I don't know why these things are happening to me—never even heard of Banbury until I arrived."

"I don't understand it either. But I trust my husband and Mr. Carter's judgment. Your Mr. Stevens seems an excellent man."

I was glad to be hidden where my blush couldn't be seen.

"I've left a clean gown for you hanging on the screen. Do you see it?"

"I thank you."

"The maid has arrived with tea—I will return in a few minutes. Do help yourself."

I would be alone? How I dreaded the thought.

She must have sensed my apprehension.

"Goodwyn Abbey is heavily guarded. You've nothing to fear."

I slipped from the cooling water, dried and dressed in a gown much more to my taste than the ones Lady Camden had chosen —then poured tea. I almost felt returned to normal other than being very tired from the long night.

In those quiet few moments, I found myself pining like a schoolgirl for Ewan. If Father were here, he would smile broadly and make a joke of it. I laughed, imagining what he would say.

How I missed the twinkle in his eyes...

Chapter Twelve

After a restless nap in one of the guest rooms, it was time for a late luncheon. A rushed affair, though I was relieved to be by Ewan's side again. The good vicar had also arrived, and drew Ewan and I aside for a private talk in the library.

Did we know the seriousness of the marriage state? Did we understand the lifelong vows we were about to make? Indeed, we did.

Ewan's hand covered my own as he answered in the affirmative.

A short while later, the magistrate arrived, hoping to gain assistance from Lord Sherborne to search for Lady Camden's mysteriously missing cousin and solicitor.

Twas the very same man who had come the night the stranger died, only this time, in not such a blustery mood over the interruption of his holiday. Instead, lines creased around his eyes and mouth—stress hung about him like those who'd abandoned the fox hunt.

I could only imagine the shrieking fits that ensued when our absence had been discovered. But we could not stay there—I could not stay, that is. Lady Camden's Hogmanay superstition had no doubt resurrected for a time before they assumed we'd eloped. Escaped, more like.

The magistrate approached me before he left Goodwyn Abbey. "I am glad that you are safe, Miss Hartford. You are in the right hands." He glanced at the gentlemen standing by the doorway. "Do you pray, my dear?"

I nodded.

"Will you spare a prayer for me? The village has never endured such mayhem." He tipped his hat. "Good day."

I curtsied as he left.

"Will he give my whereabouts away?" And did he know that someone had attempted to murder me twice?

Lord Sherborne shook his head. "Nor will anyone here. However, after your wedding tomorrow, you must be on your way."

"On my way? What do you mean?"

Ewan tucked my hand in his arm. "I'll explain the plan soon."

Leaving Butterton Hall had been the right thing to do, but I wondered...how did the housekeeper fare? Had the people who tried to murder me in my sleep threatened her in some way? Enough to sabotage her heart and cause collapse? Apparently, her moodiness hadn't been directed at me.

A dread thought entered my mind. Had her life also been at stake?

Her grim expression and listless posture assured me that she bore no fondness towards Lady Camden's cousin. None whatsoever. She wasn't happy, no, but there was something else. She, too, was afraid.

The never ending circle of questions chased my thoughts, a hound on the scent of a fox, the fox nowhere to be seen. How could any of this be true? Unless the fox were found, the chase wouldn't end.

I perched on the settee as another steaming cup of fragrant tea was placed in my hands. I drank and swallowed on a prayer. *Lord, do your justice...*

Indeed, how did a poor vicar's daughter from a rural village end up embroiled in such intrigues and scandal?

A gentle soul, a large boyish man, entered the room and stood before me clutching a bouquet—of paper flowers? His dark hair grew like a bushy mane, his vest hung askew over an unlaced shirt. No cravat to be seen. His lopsided smile made me forget my fears.

"We won't let this lamb get lost, eh, Zander?" He glanced at Lord Sherborne briefly as he shoved the flowers toward me. "Never get lost in the wood again." His face grew serious as I accepted the beautiful paper creations from his large hands. "I been lost once." He looked around. "We all been lost once—at one time or 'nother. But Zander finds us." He smiled again before scampering from the room.

Lord Sherborne laughed. "He's taken a liking to your horse, Stevens. You'll not find a better servant to the beast."

Ewan lowered next to me. "I am grateful to him."

Lady Sherborne inspected my flowers. "He couldn't rest until he'd made these for you. 'Every bride ought to have flowers for her wedding,' he said."

And he was right. "He is a kind soul."

"Oh yes. He brings much joy to Goodwyn. I cannot imagine life here without him." Lady and Lord Sherborne exchanged a loving glance.

I wondered at this couple who seemed to adore one another. I think it must have been the same with my parents when my mother was alive. Father wasn't afraid to speak of the dead. He'd spoke of her often, and fondly. He'd wanted me to know her. Love her as he did.

The young man called Matthew stepped into the drawing room where we had gathered. Tall, lean, and strong. I'd seen him on New Year's Eve. He was Banbury's heir? His arms were folded and he didn't seem altogether amused.

Lord Sherborne sat opposite of Ewan and I. "Someone took a crack at Matthew yesterday while riding to the village."

Dear God. When would this end?

"It's not only the people who were involved in Banbury's schemes that are in danger, but anyone connected to him at all."

I startled. "But I am not connected—not in the least!"

Lord Sherborne drew his hand over his short, dark beard. "Perhaps your father was, without your knowing it."

"Impossible." He'd been too busy with the daily work of shepherding his church. With weddings, baptisms, burials—and coming alongside people going through difficulties between those sacred happenings. "I'd never heard his name before coming to Butterton." And I certainly never saw any correspondence with his name. I'd gone through everything meticulously after Father had died.

"Unfortunately, he often worked through other gentlemen or used an alias name."

"Oh?" I couldn't think straight.

"I believe we are dealing with a wild card."

"Wild card?" What was he implying?

"Madness."

That word again. The one I'd thought of when my gown had been destroyed.

Lord Sherborne stood and paced. "Someone so beset with grief and bitterness, they will attempt to destroy any connection to Banbury." He paused. "And somehow, he knows who they are. I can only conclude that this person had an intimate understanding of the inner workings of Banbury's schemes." He looked to the ceiling as if appealing to God. "And has suffered greatly as a result. Mark my words, there is nothing more dangerous than a wounded wolf."

Ewan scooted to the edge of his seat. "But why is this happening particularly in Butterton?"

"Whatever our surprise New Year's guest has hidden, I imagine. Whoever is committing these crimes must also desire treasure. If indeed that's what it is."

I queried. "No one seems to know who the man was...do you?"

Lord Sherborne shook his head. "Never seen him before in my life."

"Camden's housekeeper—"

"Yes. A conundrum, that. Dr Rillian remains by her side, but he's not learned anything of value. Perhaps he can get her to speak."

"I pray these are but assumptions, but I agree. The deaths are uncanny. Mr. Chinworth's murder, while shocking, was not entirely a surprise—as we had discussed."

"But...why go after me?"

Lord Sherborne took a deep breath. "My dear, the attempts on your life may not actually be about you."

"I don't understand."

"Hold fast, Miss Hartford. The truth will out and you will be free of this tragic nonsense. I promise."

How long would it take?

Ewan took my hand and squeezed. "We'll get through this together."

His expression carried an assurance I wanted to believe. "What will your father think when he hears that you've left your post?" Would he have to return? Where would I go?

His lips lifted in a smile. "Ah, that. I didn't tell you, but my father released me from duty a few days ago. His letter arrived before the fox hunt. Said that further involvement would complicate our business. He will focus merely on the court case of that inheritance and leave Camden's employ altogether."

"Camden will have to find a new solicitor?" A good sign perhaps?

"That he will."

"Now for the plan." His thumb stroked his ring on my finger. "After the ceremony in the morning, we will depart for London. My young siblings are going to be ecstatic to discover I've got a beautiful wife."

I blushed at the words. I was going to be a wife... His.

A handsome couple entered the drawing room. Matthew jumped from his seat, shouting, "Master Carter!" he bowed almost reverently. "Mrs. Carter." He took her hand and smiled.

The gentleman owned a confident gait, yet carried an aura of kindness like everyone else at Goodwyn.

He responded, "I expect you're ready to return to Wyndhouse for more training?"

"More than ready."

Mr. Carter patted his shoulder. "That's what I like to hear."

I'd heard about what he'd had to endure—so much for someone so young.

Lady Sherborne stepped forward and introduced us. The ladies begged informality. I was to call them Elaina and Emma. Such an offer had never been made from the gentry. I felt honored by their friendship.

A maid offered a biscuit from the tray. I glanced her way. I recognized her. Mary. The missing maid from Butterton Hall.

She lowered her eyes and dipped a curtsy. "Miss."

"I'm glad to see that no harm has come to you."

"Yes, miss."

She moved to the next guest, and out of the room as quickly as possible. Thank God, she was in a good, safe place.

Lord Sherborne waited until she'd exited the room before speaking. "Came to us from Butterton Hall, frightened. Said she wouldn't work for anyone else and 'knows who it was' but refuses to say." He grimaced. "She doesn't want to bring the Hogmanay curse down upon Goodwyn Abbey."

"Other members of the household staff have been frightened as well," Ewan said.

"She went missing after my attack in the stables."

The entire room stalled as the butler entered, announcing a gentleman. "Mr. Tobias Chinworth, sir."

Tobias Chinworth? I was curious to see the man whose father had been recently murdered. I turned to see him.

Dark and unshaven, he stood at the entry. Wait... Hadn't he always appeared unshaven? My heart sped. Memories tumbled. I knew this man. I knew him well.

Only his name wasn't Tobias Chinworth. It was Arthur Melling. A man my father had sent packing mere months before his death.

Chapter Thirteen

I stood and walked towards him, ready to confront the gentleman who had left so much scandal behind him in Chilham. Ewan followed, always there for support. "Tobias Chinworth? Or, is it Arthur Melling? Or have you yet another name by which you are known?"

Tobias paled. He looked thinner, weaker. But yes, the very same man I'd known but a few years ago.

Ewan turned to me. "Jane? What are you talking about? You know this man?"

I didn't know if I should be furious at facing him again, or stunned that he was the infamous Tobias Chinworth, a man to be pitied. The loss of a father was utterly difficult. I knew.

His face reddened and he stumbled for words.

"What's this, cousin?" Mr. Carter moved to Tobias's side. "Past catching up with you?" He glanced to me as Ewan took my hand in his own.

Tobias's expression tightened as he bowed, "Miss Hartford. I owe you my deepest apology. I regret what I was in Chilham. More than you can possibly know."

Heat flooded my countenance. I'd made a spectacle—an embarrassment. How often had Father refrained the warning not to hold a man's past against him? That each day was a new day swept clean? Though he'd repented on his knees, he was sent packing—Father begging him never to return. I'd been so angry then. Regardless that he'd apologized. Sometimes words were not enough.

Mr. Carter squinted and folded his arms. All seriousness. "What *exactly* were you doing in Chilham?"

Tobias's brow wrinkled, his visage one of deep concern. I'd added a burden to his troubles. "Please, gentleman, may we talk in private?"

"Ah, yes," said Lord Sherborne. "To my study."

The men left us to ourselves for nearly an hour. The mantle clock ticked the time away as sewing and knitting had been brought out. More tea was served, and all I could do was weave and unweave my fingers in a nervous pattern.

To think that Arthur Melling was Tobias Chinworth, that he was here now, and that his father had been tied to the Banbury scandal. Was he also? Did he play a part in the misdeeds of so many? I wouldn't doubt it, and yet, there was something about his demeanor that gave me pause.

For starters, he'd apologized right away—in front of everyone too. He hadn't denied my words but owned them. The man that I'd known wouldn't have done that. He had changed.

Mrs. Carter, Emmaline, quietly recounted to me the tragic deaths of his brothers. All news to me.

"He is the only one left to care for his sister—and his nephew, wherever the poor child may be."

Elaina adjusted her shawl. "Yes. We daily pray for the babe's safe return." She looked at Emma. "Meanwhile, your sister-in-law works wonders with Cecily. I do believe she and Tobias may have formed an...attachment." Her meaning was clear.

Emma smiled. "Tobias has been writing to Joseph. I saw glimmers of a true gentleman while I stayed at Mayfield. I am so glad to hear that he chases wisdom with ferocity. I pray that he will one day understand the true depths of God's forgiveness."

Elaina nodded. "An undeserved grace, to be sure. But yes, I do pray the same. He is very hard upon himself."

I spoke up. "Perhaps he has much to make up for." I could think of several instances. Shopkeepers that went unpaid. A ruined reputation or two of innocent young women.

Elaina paused her sewing. "To carry the weight of his father's sins along with his own is a burden, to be sure. It's too heavy for anyone to carry alone. Too difficult for anyone to redeem themselves. Impossible."

Well-said. This vicar's daughter had been put in her place. Was true. Only Christ's work could redeem anyone and the doings of the past.

Ewan returned for me. "Quick. You must come—there are things you need to hear."

My heart sped in a nervous thumping as we hurried down a long, low hall. He led me into the study, where the gentlemen stood about the room, seriousness carved into their faces. He settled me beside the fire, yet the men remained standing. "You may have been surprised to see him, Jane, but his purpose in coming here today was entirely for your sake. Truly."

"Indeed?" I risked a glance in his direction. How could that be?

Lord Sherborne perched on the edge of his large desk. "We've discovered a connection. Finally."

Apprehension simmered. My father was not the kind of man to be involved in intrigues of any sort. Ever. His life, his ministry, and his every purpose had been intent on one thing: serving God. Nothing less, he'd said, would satisfy. I believed him.

Tobias ran a hand through his dark hair. "When I came to Chilham, I was there at the behest of my father. I was not to be known by the Chinworth name, only Arthur Melling, as you said. I didn't suspect why until recently.

My father sent me to deliver a sealed letter to your father. The contents of which I had no knowledge. I'd been told that I could not leave Chilham without a reply. Your father read the letter, handed it back to me, and refused to say a word."

"And so you stayed?"

"I had no desire to disappoint my father. He'd demanded a reply. Bid me to stay until I'd weaseled one out of him, by any means."

"What could he possibly have to do with Mr. Chinworth?" And then I realized the connection. What Ewan had tried to tell me. Once upon a time, my great-grandfather had been in line to inherit Butterton Hall. He'd lived here and was known—until he died. Or, as Ewan believed, had pretended to die.

Tobias continued. "I confess that I read the letter—though it made little sense to me. My father spoke of an attempt to repair a long-standing breach. A desire to help the rightful owner back into his place in society. He had a plan if only Reverend Hartford was willing."

"I take it he was not willing."

"Not in the least."

I remember Father's emphatic voice filtering through the crack in his study door—then, in the next moment, the cocksure Arthur Melling went striding out the door with a wide grin. *I'll be back, good vicar. You may count on it.* He'd winked at me...

What nerve, I remembered thinking.

"So I stayed in Chilham. I'm not proud of how I behaved, Miss Hartford. I was bored and had nothing good to put my hands to. I meant to ingratiate myself with your father to gain an answer—and in turn, gain my own father's approval." He shook his head. "I nearly failed on both accounts."

Instead, he'd ingratiated himself with me. A sorry business. But never gaining his own father's approval? Truly sad.

My expression must have told my feelings. Tobias held his hands up, palms out. "I do not need pity. I am beyond that." He refolded him arms. "Though I'd read the letter meant for your father, I didn't understand the gist of it. And didn't care. When your father gave me the boot, so to speak, he finally agreed to send a message back. The contents of which I was ignorant until recently."

Ewan pulled a chair beside me and took my hand.

"Over the months that Father has been sequestered in the gaol house, I've been going through his papers. Piece by piece. I transcribed everything he told me about his past. Above all, he desired absolution." His face grew pained. "I recorded everything from his involvement in that terrible coach crash," his eyes flicked to Mr. Carter, "to his earliest dealings with Banbury." He swallowed. "I found the letter your father had sent to him through me."

Lord Sherborne picked up the parchment from his desk. "This letter."

Yes, that was my father's handwriting penned in tight, straight lines.

"And then I heard you'd come to Butterton." His hand drew through his hair again. "The poor cousin to Lady Camden, a vicar's daughter. I wondered how much you knew. Once I'd read your father's response, I understood that the family line had been disrupted in some strange way. In what way, I was ignorant. Not until Lord Camden came begging one evening."

"On December thirtieth?"

His eyes squinted. "How did you know?"

Ewan spoke up. "Always been curious why he was not in attendance to greet Lady Camden's long-lost cousin that they so greatly desired to be a part of the family. As his solicitor, I advised him to keep from anyone in the Chinworth family until I could sort out his involvement. Needless to say, Lord Camden did not listen."

Mr. Carter next sauntered across the room and tossed a piece of wood onto the fire. "What did he beg for?"

"My father had some sort of a hold over Lord Camden. I hesitate to use the word blackmail, but," he shrugged, "maybe it was. Anyway, Camden came begging for a particular box of family papers that had belonged to his wife. He made up some excuse that my father had been interested in historic family genealogies around Butterton." He shook his head. "Father was never interested in any but the Chinworth family line."

Ewan dipped his chin. "Did you give it to him?"

"No," he shrugged, "In sorting through his many papers—I'd hoped to find something that would help my father's case, not hurt it—and no. I found no such box. Lord Camden became belligerent. Started tearing through the room."

I could sense tension and fear emanating from Tobias. His teeth gritted together as he spoke through them. "He said something about making a trade."

"What kind of trade?"

"My young nephew for those documents."

"The baby?" The one who disappeared after his parents had died?

"Yes. My brother's legitimate child. The Chinworth heir. It is no secret that we've been searching high and low for him."

Mr. Carter's fist balled into his hand. "The miscreant knows where he is? Dear God."

Ewan spoke up. "The letter that I found, and the other examples that point to Jane being the heiress of Butterton Hall, were taken from my office but a few days ago."

Lord Sherborne nodded. "He must have suspected that in your digging you'd found something of interest. Especially since you were the one to incite an invitation for Miss Hartford to come."

Ewan's arm went about my shoulder, a welcome warmth. "We can assume that what Chinworth held was information concerning Jane's great-grandfather. Perhaps it's possible that he even knew the man, as Chinworth was of an age. Maybe in his youth?"

"Very possible," Sherborne said.

"Chinworth made an effort to right a wrong." Mr. Carter had pulled a dagger from somewhere and was sharpening it on a stone. Soft, foreboding scrapes.

"There is a warning to the phrase 'let the sleeping dog lie'." I said.

"I'm afraid," Sherborne said, "that the dog never slept. It's hard to hold onto a truth and live out a lie. I wonder how Camden sleeps at night?"

I shook my head. "As we thought, I am a threat to Lord Camden's living. And by dying, I'd be out of the way. I was, after all, the end of my family line."

Tobias pulled an envelope from his pocket. "In father's desk in his private rooms, I found this."

Lord Sherborne snatched it from his hand and opened the missive. "It wasn't Chinworth blackmailing Camden. It was Banbury. But of course. He delighted in holding the Ton in the palms of his hands, dangling them like puppets from strings." He handed the letter to Ewan. "Camden is deeply in debt. Coffers that once held plenty are depleted. Banbury, no doubt used Camden's money, among that of others, to fund his cache of prize money."

"Prize money?" An inconceivable thought. Whatever did he mean?

"People who weren't interested in joining his games were sometimes forced to play – or pay a very high price. Right or wrong, money is always a motivation for doing a thing, is it not?"

I rubbed my eyes as exhaustion tugged.

"Miss Hartford." Lord Sherborne approached. "Take courage. Banbury is dead these many months. Your father, God rest his soul, refused to play the wretched game. You may take comfort in that."

"Game?"

Tobias nodded. "My father sought to restore the good vicar to his rightful place in society, but it came with a caveat. He'd forever be in Banbury's sights."

Lord Sherborne placed my father's letter to Chinworth in my hands. I scanned the contents that listed the attributes of the life God had set before him...

It pains me to leave my daughter poor, but I trust in her Heavenly Father, who owns the cattle on a thousand hills to care for her more than I ever could. Using her good name to pressure me into acceptance is an ill thing, sir. I do not know you, yet I am sure that my grandfather's path, while not of the innocent turn, did turn me onto a path ordered by God. Of this path, I will not turn aside for any fortune. His will be done.

God save you,

Edward Hartford.

Tears slipped down my cheeks at his answer to Chinworth's offer. This truth, at its core, had never been more prevalent to me. How people sought to gain fortune regardless of lives! To think that the price of a soul might cost a mere pound. Shameful.

Ewan handed me his handkerchief as I swiped my tears away. I cleared my throat, "Lord Camden desires the papers in exchange for your brother's child? Only you don't know where to find what he desires."

"Correct." Tobias finally sat, exhaling a long breath.

"The fact that Lord Camden would bargain with a babe's life shows the seriousness of the proof of inheritance. And the man's wickedness." Ewan held me tighter. "I know you do not care about gaining a title and Butterton Hall..."

I pressed a hand to my heart. "The child's life is what matters. My so-called claim is meaningless."

Ewan rose from my side. "Within months, Camden will be challenged in court. Wouldn't be surprised if this incredible situation rises to the surface."

"Does it have to?" I worried what exposure of the truth might mean for all of us.

"It may, whether we want it to or not."

Chapter Fourteen

"But why did Lord Camden faint when he heard of Chinworth's death?" His reaction still seemed immoderate.

"Perhaps he hoped the man would reveal where the box was hidden before he died."

"And the rest of the gentlemen that fled the fox hunt?"

Lord Sherborne paced to the hearth and back to his desk. "Banbury's tentacles stretched far and wide. If Banbury was blackmailing Camden through Chinworth, then mayhap he did the same to others attending the hunt." He turned about to face the room. "Chinworth was put into an impossible position by Banbury, holding the trespasses of others as a means of controlling them. Chinworth's recent actions have been an attempt to right many wrongs. But one cannot salvage guilt by practicing further deceit."

Mr. Carter finished the thought. "Only by complete honesty can anyone attempt such."

"So, the deaths of those connected to Banbury aren't necessarily..." I couldn't finish the thought. Was too much to take in. It hurt too much to contemplate.

"Oh no. They are entirely tied to the case. Chinworth may have had more to do with Banbury than we knew, but someone is out there cutting participants down, one by one—for their safety? Or is it madness? I don't know. I do believe that Camden fears not only his position but for his life."

"What can we do?" I was still confused as to why I was a target. Indeed, all fingers seemed to point to Camden as my assailant. There was motive and opportunity, to be sure. But something didn't set right.

Matthew cracked his knuckles. "Maybe get him to confess?"

Ewan shook his head. "He'd never do that. Stubborn man."

"I say we pay a visit to Butterton Hall." Mr. Carter sheathed the dagger. "Ply him about the baby. And the stranger that seemed to know his name. Give him a chance to tell the truth." He picked at a button on his sleeve. "Where is the body, the man buried yet?"

Lord Sherborne grinned. "Much to my household staff's chagrin, I've kept the man in my ice house. The magistrate is to send an artist to take his likeness on the morrow. Then, we may bury him."

Mr. Carter said, "Indeed. I ought to take a look at him." He turned to me. "My pardon, Miss Hartford. An unsavory task."

How many bedside or death ministrations had I helped with over the years? Too many to count. "I've seen many a deceased person. I quit squirming from such viewings a long time ago."

Lord Sherborne shrugged into his coat. "Shall we? I do not know him, but perhaps at second glance, one of you might recognize him." He sent a pointed look to Matthew.

"Yes, Zander. I will go this time." Matthew looked at me. "Maybe I can be of some help, even in a small way."

Lord Sherborne touched his shoulder. "You've been a tremendous help—we wouldn't have come this far without you, that is for certain."

Ewan took my hand. "I'll see you back to the ladies."

"No. I want to come."

"You are sure?"

I nodded. It was my duty.

The icehouse was bone-chilling cold. Colder than the frozen out-of-doors. Lord Sherborne led us around the blocks of ice to a tarp-covered pallet. I stood back as he lifted the shroud from the man's face. The gentlemen shifted forward to see.

There was a moment of silence, and then, Matthew spoke. "I've seen him." His voice strangled. "He's one of the men from Cornwall. One of the men who beat me." He turned away and ran toward the house.

Lord Sherborne recovered the tarp over the dead man. "Tis why I kept the body for so long. I knew if Matthew recognized him, then others in Cornwall would too. Whatever he buried came from one of Banbury's wrecks. Mayhap, the Dawes Shipping wreck..."

Ewan quoted the man's last words. "None shall have it. No Banbury gets the last word. Not when I gone through the trouble." He clenched a fist. "A curse, it is. A curse..."

"Even one such as he fought against Banbury, even at the point of death." Mr. Carter led the way out.

Tobias punched the palm of his hand with his fist. "Lord Camden emulates Banbury. Bargaining with a life—a babe's no less. It isn't to be borne!"

Ewan led the way out but Tobias paused at my side.

I had to speak with him. Offer some sort of olive branch. "I am sorry, Mr. Mell—Chinworth. You've lost so much..."

His eyes shuttered closed for a moment. "I have. And yet, I find life filling up where the empty places have been."

Did he speak of the attachment Elaina alluded to?

"I keep praying for my nephew's return. Begging God. Day after day."

Unceasing prayer. "He hears you."

"I don't deserve to be heard—yet this is what the vicar tells me is His grace." He took a deep breath. "I am glad you are here, despite the circumstances." He offered a small smile. "I offended you deeply while in Chilham."

"I forgive you."

He bowed.

Ewan responded in kind. "If you need a solicitor..."

"Of course." He shook Lord Sherborne's hand—then Mr. Carter's. "The gaol released my father's body. He is to be buried on the morrow. After the wedding."

Mr. Carter clapped him on the back. "I will stand with you, cousin."

"Thank you."

We watched Tobias ride away before going back inside Goodwyn.

Lord Sherborne plunked down into a chair without ceremony, no doubt tired from the long night. "He will do well, Carter. I have no doubt."

Mr. Carter folded him arms. "I never thought I'd see the day. Thank God I have."

Supper was served soon after. I found myself at the table of friends—companions—who despite intent darkness that had fallen over Butterton, shone with the joy of ones who had already conquered difficulty. Indeed, they had. They gave me hope that though my life had been at stake, and may still be, the struggle would one day end.

I glanced at Ewan. Love would be the end result. And friends I wouldn't have otherwise.

Near the end of the meal, the dining hall door flung open.

"Doctor Rillian!" Elaina rushed to him.

Bent and out of breath, he held a bleeding arm close to his side. "Camden has fled. I know not where."

"Was it he that wounded you?"

"No. Some blackguard had been lying in wait—in the wood."

"Could it have been Camden?"

"The man can't aim very well. And in the dark? No. Wasn't him. Though I wouldn't put it past him to hire out."

We gathered around him as he sank into a chair. "The housekeeper improves. Indeed, she rallies. I left her side to check on the swooning Camdens. Lady S. sleeps soundly. Lord S. is nowhere to be found. His room is in disarray. And half of the household, mind you, has abandoned their posts."

"Why you?"

"Perhaps it was discovered that I encouraged Miss Hartford to leave Butterton. The staff have sensitive ears, do they not?" Dr. Rillian looked at me. "It is imperative you are in safekeeping."

Ewan's hands held my shoulders. "I will not leave her side."

"Be sure that you don't."

Elaina looked to Lord Sherborne. "Someone hides in our wood?"

He nodded. "I have a watch set around Goodwyn. You are not to fear."

Mr. Carter's eyes gleamed with readiness. "I will join them."

Matthew sidled up to Dr. Rillian. "Allow me to see to your arm, doctor."

"The patient mends his healer, is that it?"

"I've learned a thing or two."

Dr. Rillian allowed Matthew to help as I was quickly sequestered in a cozy bedchamber linked with two other rooms that held Ewan in one, and Lord Sherborne in the other. My doorway had been blocked from within.

Ewan embraced me. "Sleep as much as you can. Tomorrow is a long day."

Our wedding, plus the long ride to London to his home...and family.

He kissed my forehead and released me with an intent look. He smiled and leaned against the doorway. We gazed at each other for a long moment. So many thoughts and words between us to share, yet we stayed silent.

In the morning, we would say our vows.
I hoped he wouldn't regret it.

Chapter Fifteen

Snow swept downward on the morning of our wedding. We rode to church bundled in borrowed cloaks with warm bricks at our feet. I wore a borrowed gown of soft ivory wool, and a bonnet to match. Simple, but so elegant that I felt every inch a bride.

Elaina had gifted me with a trunk full of necessities until I could safely receive my belongings from Butterton Hall. Not much remained. After my room had been ransacked, precious little had been salvageable. And the gowns Lady Camden had ordered were a bit more on the opulent side. Tacky even. I had been loathe to wear them.

Ewan handed me down with his chipped tooth smile that distracted all thinking—did he know how handsome it made him? I would never tire of that grin.

He led me to the altar where the vicar waited. With a quiet rustle, our friends took their seats in the pews. If only Father were here—if only he could have been the one presiding, his warm voice comforting me. The words we would repeat, I'd known them by heart for many years—learned on the many occasions that I had the honor of witnessing unions at the chapel in Chilham. Such dear days—and such solemn moments. Marriage was a covenant not to be broken.

I took a deep breath at that knowledge.

Ewan, my protector spoke first, then I. With hands clasped, the cool air warmed by the intent of the promises we repeated. Could I cherish this man? Would he cherish me? We promised to do that—and more. By the grace of God, I would. As would he.

At the end, my new husband lowered his head to mine and kissed me, gathering me close. "Little did I know that when I implored the Camdens to bring you here, that you'd become my precious bride. I believe God sent you to me."

As I believed God had sent Ewan when I needed him most.

We signed the register. There—our names were irrevocably linked together under the sight of God and His church. How well I liked seeing our names side by side!

I hoped to gain another journal. I should like to record the good that has occurred as a result of the danger. To look back upon when life becomes difficult in my future. I will be able to recount God's goodness, and maybe, my children will see the testimony of it too.

"You must leave quickly now." Lord Sherborne shook Ewan's hand. "I'm sending Matthew with you." He nodded to the young man leaning against the doorframe. "He has business to attend at the Banbury estate. I'll join him next week."

Elaina and Emma embraced me as we said a hasty goodbye.

"Come, Jane." Ewan pulled me through the back door where the carriage waited. He handed me in, and as soon as Matthew was settled, the coach moved onward.

My new life lay ahead. One not tied up in the intrigue of tangled fortunes or fearsome doings at Butterton Hall.

The Sherborne's well-sprung carriage moved at a steady pace, so steady that Matthew fell asleep soon after departing. Ewan's arm slid around my shoulders and drew me closer as the hot brick beneath our feet had cooled.

He pressed a kiss to my temple and made a contented sound. I hoped our lives could indeed move forward with peace.

I thought of what I'd learned in my history books—of royalty, divided families, and the constant fight for the crown to rule a people, and by it, an empire. There were a few unfortunate souls who didn't desire what they'd inherited. And yet they were forced to fulfill what they thought was a divine call to rule. Another Jane, one Lady Jane Grey, ruled but nine days before her young life was forfeited. And before her, the young brothers— Edward and Richard—kidnapped? Murdered? Certainly never seen again.

Inheritance seemed a dangerous thing. Too often, bloodlines and brothers betray one another. I supposed my great-grandfather sought to leave that life behind. The estate came to Lady Camden in the rare circumstance that a lady might own an estate. And Lord Camden, the control of it because he was her husband.

I thought of the grand Elizabethan structure of Butterton Hall that had once housed those before me. How I'd branched off with my grandfather and father before me, but had been positioned back again. And how my life, like Lady Jane Grey's, was a threat to others. But an estate was not a kingdom. The aged structure and its gracious additions were beautiful, to be sure, but no politics, and no nation depended upon its ruler. Nay, merely a handful of tenants and dairy farms. A sleepy land of wool, milk, and cheese...

Lord Sherborne had mentioned that Camden's fortune had been all but depleted. Did his wife's potential inheritance matter enough to end my life that they may gain it? I supposed some foolish man might, in a rash moment, sell his birthright for a bowl of stew.

Ewan must have seen the concern in my eyes. He took my free hand in his own. "You have nothing to be afraid of anymore."

In that moment, I could well believe him.

After several hours, we disembarked at a rather old-looking coaching inn of half-timber and mud—and what appeared to be several levels of low ceilings. We stretched our sore muscles, so many hours spent traveling! Such a relief to be so far from danger.

The night fast approached. Ewan and I were ushered within and given a private parlor—a generous supper was soon laid before us.

We took our time, eating slowly, savoring our small wedding feast—as husband and wife. Everything had happened so fast, I realized that I no longer needed to look out for a situation. I was a *wife...* My role and position were clear.

Looking at my husband and his handsome smile, I knew I needed no other occupation. The vicar called it "Holy Matrimony". Yes—I felt the sacredness of our union already. We talked of our future together. Of never suffering loneliness again. Of his work and his plan to install us within our own home as soon as may be possible.

The innkeeper's wife led us upstairs to the door of our room with the assurance that a fire had been lit and fresh water delivered. Ewan turned the knob and stepped inside—I followed.

A man shoved past me and barred the door. Another smacked Ewan across his head. He sank to the ground as if dead. I tried to scream but a cloth had been wrapped around my mouth as I tried to reach for Ewan.

Lord Camden. No. It couldn't be!

His face was pale, his eyes wide with fright. Yet he held me fast as he gave directions to another man in the room.

A short, but brawny-looking man—a sailor? He reached for me and I glimpsed a strange tattoo scrawled against his forearm. A sea serpent. The brute quickly tied my hands in a strong, thin rope that dug deep into my wrists.

I tugged vigorously but to no avail. I'd been captured. Dear God, what was happening? Why? If I could speak, I would promise Camden that I'd disappear. He'd need never see or know me again. Would it even work? Jane Hartford, nay Jane Stevens, wanted nothing of his. Nothing.

Ewan had only been knocked unconscious. At least I hoped that to be true. I sat beside him, leaning against the bedframe praying—begging God to awaken him.

Camden bound Ewan's hands and feet, then waved to the man. "We leave. Make certain the stairway is empty."

The man grunted.

Camden had disappeared from his estate. He knew I would try to leave. He'd waited—followed us here and would enact his evil. With so much hope on my horizon, I wasn't ready to die. I wanted to be Ewan's wife for a good long while.

The brute jerked me to my feet and pushed me towards the door after Camden—I looked down at Ewan. They were leaving him. I tried to jerk away once more but he held me fast.

Before we reached the back stairway, I was tossed over his shoulder and shoved to the floor of a dark carriage. The men climbed in after me—and in a blink, the carriage sped away.

My new life, my new love lay wounded, perhaps seriously. And I would never see him again. Had I thought that I'd truly escaped this evil? That I'd record and testify God's faithfulness in this matter? I closed my eyes against tears. He would keep my soul, this I knew. I may well speak of His faithfulness face-to-face this night, my own father beside me. Twas the only thought that I could cling to. That I would see my father again.

We sped along for a few hours, my limbs grew cramped in the tiny space. The men didn't speak. I wondered why they did not end my life immediately—if that had been the intent before, why put off the inevitable?

The carriage stopped and the driver grunted as he flung the door open. "Get out here."

Camden stepped down, and the brute jerked me to my feet and tied a musty cloth around my eyes. They didn't want me to see where we were going. What did it matter if I were to die?

He dragged me behind him for several paces—I tripped many times as sand slipped into my boots. Sand—the cry of an occasional gull. We were near the sea. I could smell it, hear its roar in the distance.

I heard the clink of keys against metal, then a creak. I was shoved through a doorway while my blindfold was ripped off.

Here was a cottage. A cozy cottage with a low fire flickering in the fireplace, a lantern glowed upon the rough but clean wooden table, and two rocking chairs bespoke of simple comfort. A rug had been added to the floor and the small kitchen appeared well-endowed with every necessity for sustenance. A door opened from the other end of the cottage and a large, buxom woman appeared.

"Thought ye might be comin' this night—" she stopped cold when she saw me. "Who's this? Not the babe's mother, is it? Come to your senses, have you?"

I shook my head.

"Why ye bind her, man?"

Camden flicked his head. "Untie her."

The brute slipped a knife from a holster and cut the rope from my hands, yanked the cloth from my mouth. I winced at the release, rubbing my raw wrists and jaw.

The woman squinted at me with one eye. "Oh aye, she's a right pretty one." She grinned. "What do ye plan to do with 'er?"

A mewling cry came from the other room. "Ye've woke the poor babe." She retreated for a moment and returned with a dark-haired cherub clinging to her well-endowed hip. His eyes grew wide at the newcomers, a string of drool dripped from his chin.

The babe. Hers, perhaps?

And then I remembered Camden's bargain with Tobias. The box of papers for his nephew. This babe, hidden from his father for safekeeping, had also been taken and hidden from the entire family. He'd somehow landed in the wrong hands along the way. Tobias's desperation to find him had been palpable.

The nurse jostled him as he began to cry. "The wee rascal's teethin'."

Tobias didn't have the box of papers—couldn't find them if they existed at all. Yet Camden hadn't lied. Here was the Chinworth heir. Imprisoned with a caretaker who seemed entirely ignorant of the truth.

Camden spoke. "Give the babe to Jane, Nancy. That's right. I have something else I need you to do."

"Oh aye? I suppose he don't need feedin'." She handed me the plump child who cried harder at being separated from his sole comfort. "Right then."

Camden looked at me and lifted his brows. "Of course you know how to care for a child?"

I was so bewildered, I gave no answer. The babe reached with both arms for his nurse, his cry heightened. In truth, I hadn't much experience with infants. I'd held them on occasion while visiting bustling families about Chilham, but I'd not the fortune of having siblings—didn't even know how to change a diaper.

Camden opened the door to the cold night air and the trio left the babe and me alone. It was up to us to work out the details. The icy breeze startled the poor thing to blessed silence. The lad and I were trapped together. The Chinworth and Butterton heirs. Sequestered together as in the Tower of London, awaiting our fates. My heart sped and my hands trembled. I needed to sit and adjust the little one nearer.

Dear God...would that we could simply walk from this cottage and escape. I paced the room, getting my bearings. I peered from the windows. The brute guarded the door. Apart from those few windows, there was no other way out. Perhaps we were both to die—and God would not leave this poor child without someone to clasp him close in his last moments.

I looked at him— he was quite curious about the stranger who held him. His eyes stayed upon my face as his lips pursed in the frown from his tears. His downy soft black hair—like Tobias's, though I was certain he resembled his dead brother. Compassion enveloped me. I would love this babe until the end, if that was indeed our path.

I settled into one of the rocking chairs, pulling it close to the fire. He nestled into me as I tugged his blanket closer. I gazed upon his plump baby face, noted his tiny fingers clutched about the blanket—only desiring warmth and security. His eyelids shuttered and he slept. Tears clogged my throat. Holding a precious life so close gave way to a dream – a hope – that I might not live to see. Would Ewan and I have been blessed with children? How many? What names?

Was life and dreaming still possible? I didn't know if there was a point. Breath by breath, I had to cling to one singular hope. God was with us.

Save us, God. Save us. I would never stop praying.

I hummed a tune, softly, quietly. I hummed and hummed even until the fire died completely and I had no more strength to rock.

Chapter Sixteen

In the wee hours of the morning, I heard something shift. A distinct thunk and a shuffling sound. Had they returned? Was it time? My stomach soured. I readjusted the snuffly babe and rubbed my eyes.

The door opened, then quickly shut. My throat grew dry.

A male voice whispered, "Mrs. Stevens?"

I sat up and the babe squirmed.

"Don't be afraid. It's me. Matthew Dawes."

"Matthew?" I whispered as well. "How ever did you find me?"

"I never left you, Mrs. Stevens." He knelt before me. "Are you hurt? Are you alright?"

"I'm frightened." He'd never left my side? How was that possible?

He squeezed my shoulder. "I know how you feel. I'm going to get you out of here."

I nodded. "We have to take this babe with us. It's Chinworth's."

"We need to move quickly. I don't know when Camden will return. I've been keeping watch these many hours. I waited until that man at the door fell asleep before... well...before I..."

I reached out to him and felt his trembling hand.

"He will live, but he will be incapacitated for a time." Matthew took the baby as though he'd held tiny tots many a time. The wee one remained in a quiet, sleepy stupor—and I thanked God.

In a flash, we were outside in the freezing cold. "I'm going to need you to trust me, Mrs. Stevens. Can you do that?"

I nodded.

He handed me a dagger. The same one I'd kept on my person while at Butterton. "You left something behind. Keep it. Just in case."

I took it and strapped the belt around my waist.

"Quick now—and quiet." We slipped around the back of the house while Matthew looked in every direction. We traversed the open countryside with precious little to hide behind. I feared discovery.

Soon, we came upon the seaside village. It was still dark, but lanterns floated about here and there as its people began to stir. We came upon some large rocks and slipped behind them to rest. Matthew handed me the babe.

"We're going to make for the caves by the sea." But before we moved again, Matthew withdrew his dagger.

I followed him with such blind faith. This thin, young man—how could he possibly keep us safe? If Ewan had been easily taken down, how did we truly fare? If we were discovered, I hated to think that Matthew might lose his life for me.

How ironic. Another heir, the Banbury heir, added to the mix.

By the grace of God, we meandered and slipped through the village without notice and made our way to the caves along the coast. He sheathed his dagger and lent me his hand. "This way." He traversed the rocks as though familiar with the terrain.

Hadn't Elaina told me some of the story? That he'd hidden here, afraid for his life when she thought he'd died in the shipwreck? We must be somewhere in Cornwall.

He waved me to a large rock and bid me to shelter behind it. He entered the opening of a cave first. After a few minutes, he retrieved me. "We will be safe here."

I followed him inside where he'd already lit a small rush lamp. I sat and nearly cried with relief. My eyes burned from the cold wind, my fingers were nearly numb. I didn't have so much as a handkerchief.

"Do explain, Master Dawes, how you are here?" The last time I'd seen him, he'd taken to his quarters at the coaching inn.

"I was sent along with you to help. I didn't go to bed but scouted around the inn. Sherborne and Carter thought it would be good practice for me." He shook his head. "No one believed anything would happen to us on our way to London. We expected that Camden was in hiding—not that he would pursue you."

Matthew gathered some driftwood and started a small fire. Barely enough to warm our hands.

"I saw them take you out of the inn—and jumped onto the back of the coach. The driver didn't see me."

"You held on for hours?" I pictured his discomfort. How awful that must have been.

"I've held on for longer, Mrs. Stevens." A shadow flicked across his eyes. He'd endured much, at such a young age. "When I was sure that Camden hadn't harmed you yet, I kept watch until they left—and the guard slept." He shrugged. "And here we are."

"They attacked Ewan. I think he's alive, but..." Hot tears flowed down my cheeks.

"Hope for the best. 'Tis all we can do except to pray, of course."

I nodded. He was right.

We huddled around the tiny fire, all of us heirs. Not only a living but an unknown fate. Oh, the irony. But I would not trade this cave for the Tower of London. No indeed. I thanked God for sending Matthew.

Could it be that what Camden meant for evil, God intended as a rescue mission for the innocent life that I cradled in my arms? I hoped upon hope that could be true.

Hours later, Matthew took him from me and I stretched my sore limbs. Then I remembered. The twenty pounds that Ewan had given me when I'd first arrived in Butterton—I'd taken to wearing it in my shoe. There it remained.

I squeezed my eyes shut in thankfulness. We had money enough to get out of this place.

"Matthew? How much money do you carry?"

He shook his head. "Naught but a few pounds and shillings. We'll have to conserve it for food."

"You won't believe what I have in my shoe..." When I showed him, he smiled—and his eyes lit with hope.

"Thank God. I didn't particularly care for another adventure in these caves. Though in hindsight, I see that God was preparing me to do far more than I ever imagined." His voice trailed away.

He'd been training, I recalled, to defend himself and protect others. Mr. Carter operated a school of sorts—and Matthew was his pupil. If his difficulties had not occurred, would he have been bold enough to latch onto the carriage—then rescue me from Camden's grasp?

"First, we are going to have to steal some clothing from the wash line." He grinned. "Don't worry, I'll restore what we've taken. But leaving looking like this will make us stand out too much."

I glanced down at my dress—smeared and streaked with mud, damp from our trek. "I suppose you are right, but shouldn't we purchase what we need?"

"In this village, Mrs. Stevens? No indeed. The last thing we need to do is run into Camden." He tamped out the fire with his boot. "I aim to see you and the babe safely out of this place."

My captor would expect me to go back to Ewan—back the way I came. Maybe even back to Butterton where my friends were. But no, I knew in my gut that we weren't to return there. Or even go to London where I might show up unexpectedly to Ewan's family house.

I knew where I must go—to Chilham, where my life and history began. Back to Sir Jones and his wife. They would know what to do and how to proceed.

I pressed a hand against my heart. If only I could know if Ewan lived. Hope still burned bright.

"We have a long journey ahead, Matthew."

"Where are we to go? On to London, perhaps?"

"To Chilham…"

He nodded slowly and gazed beyond me through the mouth of the cave, where the sky began to lighten and the sea crashed endlessly against the rocks. "I have no love for Cornwall, but Mrs. Stevens, Chilham is a very long journey from here. Clear on the other side of the English Channel's coast.

"I know it."

"You are determined?"

"I have a feeling that we are meant to go there." God was prompting me.

"Very well." He exhaled a long breath. He'd already been so brave and would continue to be. He had a determination in his countenance not common among those at seventeen years of age. Indeed, I believed him quite the man already. "Before we launch into our expedition, I want to pray for God's protection and guidance." He reached to me with his large, dirty hand and I gripped it with my own.

We held on, silently appealing to God. While I was grateful to be out of danger, I knew how quickly that could change.

He squeezed my hand and rose from the cave floor. "You stay here. I will return shortly with clothing." He glanced at the babe. "And some milk for him."

God grant him success.

I waited for what seemed a few hours. The sun had risen, peering bleakly through the clouds. The babe stirred and blinked in the strange surroundings. He snuggled closer to me. Was a good thing the tike didn't seem to be able to walk yet and had remained calm and comforted.

But the babe needed changing—I dearly hoped Matthew would bring something to wrap him in. I pulled the wet diaper off and tossed it to the side.

I imagined how furious Camden would be when he found his bargaining chip missing along with his dear wife's cousin. To think that the man wanted me to come to Butterton only to dispose of me...how the thought soured in my mind!

Finally, Matthew returned. I hadn't realized that I'd been holding my breath. I'd been afraid without admitting it, that he would be prevented from returning and that we'd be left alone.

"Here." He tossed me a bundle. "Some extra cloth for the baby."

"Thank you. You're a good man, Matthew Dawes."

Blush crept up his collar. One day, I was sure his dedication to defending the helpless would make him very attractive to someone.

"There is a stagecoach down the road a few miles. One open road, I hate to say. But I think we shall manage if you wear your bonnet low and keep the babe well covered."

"Camden might recognize you if we crossed his path."

"That old man? Never paid me a glance except for when his pockets began to empty. Begging for Banbury money, he is. Except I have little control over it yet. Sherborne helps with that until I come of age." His lips curved into a frown. "I'd be too valuable to cut down. Not that I want to be. Valued at my inheritance, that is. Or cut down." A giggle escaped his throat. "Had enough of that."

He pulled a corked bottle from his coat. "Best feed the babe before we begin."

"Where did you manage to steal this from?" Couldn't help admiring his ingenuity, I uncorked the milk as the boy clutched the bottle between both hands and drank hungrily. At his age, he might have had some porridge too. I hoped the milk would hold out until we found more.

He winked. "I have a fisher wife friend, just down on the wharf. She's a good sort. Saved me when I was dying."

"Would she help us?"

"I don't want to bring more trouble on her doorstep than what's already been brought. Times have been hard for her. I left her with my pound notes, seeing as we have yours."

"Well done."

"And she gave us these." He pulled two small loaves from his coat pocket.

My stomach squeezed in hunger but gratitude multiplied.

Chapter Seventeen

Matthew coached me before leaving the cave. "Don't run, or rush, but move along at a steady pace."

Of course, he was right. We would play the part of a young couple with our sweet child. Perfectly normal. Not at all uncommon in these parts. If approached, I was not to speak, for fear my accent might give me away.

By some miracle, we made it down the long, sandy road to the coach stop and found plenty of room on board—only one other passenger besides us. An old gentleman with a rather nasty cough.

When the man had lolled to sleep, Matthew confessed. "When I was in the village, I saw Camden."

"How did he seem?"

"Ill. The man stumbled about like he was drunk. Maybe he was."

"He didn't see you?"

"No."

"The carriage is slowing, why is it slowing?"

We'd stopped. The door opened. Camden. I turned my face to the window and kept the babe turned. Matthew did the same. But it didn't matter. I knew we'd been found.

The door shut as he settled into his seat with a grunt. What should we do? Matthew pulled a newspaper from his coat pocket and opened it wide to hide his face. How I wished I might hide behind it too.

The coach shifted forward and we made our way to Plymouth—the first stop. Was he armed? Did he carry a weapon?

I wanted to confront him. Demand answers. Dole out retribution for wreaking such endless havoc in my life. But Matthew's instructions stayed me. However, it was only a matter of time before the babe would be recognized. He grew antsy and wanted to move about. I couldn't blame him.

My stomach had become a pit of nerves and worry.

The older gentleman coughed and tapped Matthew's newspaper with his silver-topped cane. "Young man. I say, young man. Lower your paper."

Matthew did not comply.

"I know who you are, there's no hiding the fact."

Matthew lowered his newspaper but a fraction. "Do you, sir?"

I risked a glance at the man.

"You're Banbury's heir." The man tapped his nose. "These parts haven't been kind to you, have they? Come now. What do you here?"

Camden swiveled around and pulled at my cloak. "I knew it!"

The old gentleman slapped Camden with his cane. "Have you lost your senses, man? Leave the woman be."

"She is my cousin. I have every right." He rubbed his arm.

I inched away.

"Do you?" The man laughed. "Not so, from what I hear." His expression grew grim. "The shores of Cornwall have enough scandal for you to bring more of it to my doorstep. "What are you hiding, Camden?"

"How do you know me?" Camden paled as the tips of his ears grew red.

"I make it my business to know any society that steps foot upon my village." The man's hearty laugh changed into a cough. "What kind of contraband do you dare to hide here? An heir? Or two or three? My gracious, man, you are industrious." His face drew a grim line. "The locals, they relish in wrecking and stealing. A life for some liquor, a death for a dram. But what can a babe be to you?" His smile revealed wide, glinting teeth. "Must you resort to trading in babies? How do you plan to use all three heirs to your advantage? Hmm?"

Camden sputtered. "You don't understand."

"I understand more than you wish I did." The man removed a blade from his cane and held it to Camden. "I've been instructed to take you in. The crown has a few...inquiries."

Matthew had lowered his paper.

"Master Dawes, do rap the ceiling."

Matthew did as bid.

Camden glanced at me, sweat gleaming across his forehead, despite the cold. "Jane, do tell the man that I have done nothing. That I have not harmed you or the child."

I showed him my raw wrists instead. "Would that were true. You've tried to kill me, and more than once." My voice was loud and clear.

"No, no, no! You have it wrong, my dear!"

The carriage stopped.

"So I was dreaming when I saw you attack Ewan and haul me here? On my wedding day, no less."

"Tut, tut, Camden. Your transgressions pile up, rather."

"Was the only way to save you! You don't understand! They were going to—" he swallowed, looking ill. "If I didn't take you, they were going to kill you. I had to get you out of there or you would be dead right now, girl. You can be sure of that."

His expression bade me to believe him. Tears glistened. "They were going to kill me and my wife too."

The old man cocked his head. "Who, Camden?"

He puffed a great breath of air.

The man laughed in response.

"The same that killed Chinworth. The same that ended the lives of the others. The same that—" He slashed his hand through the air, "that ended Brown's life. And who knows how many others."

Brown? Was that the name of the stranger that had died at New Year's? "Did you try to kill Dr. Rillian?"

"No! I didn't know—is he wounded?"

The man might be lying, but I sincerely couldn't tell.

"Why did you try to bargain with this child? You had no right!"

"I was threatened. And that is all I'm going to say until I talk with my solicitor."

"Your solicitor, my husband, is wounded—or dead, for all I know. Thanks to you."

Panic flitted across his face as my heart pounded. Could I trust this man's words? If Camden had tried to save me, who, indeed, wanted me out of the way?

The door opened and a man I hadn't seen before stood waiting. A runner?

Camden stepped down. "I wish you would believe me."

"I have no reason to, sir."

He bowed his head. "I give up. I am tired. So very tired."

The older gentleman followed him out. "Be on your way, Master Dawes, Mrs. Stevens. I shall send word to Lord Sherborne that I've seen you." He winked "A rather fortuitous chance meeting, do you not think?"

Matthew nodded. "Thank you, sir—"

He brushed his hand at the query. "Better you not know." He shut the coach door. "Get thee safe." He pulled a pistol and kit from his bag. "You know how to shoot, I expect?"

"Yes, sir."

"Well done, then. Take it." He handed them through the window and shouted to the driver. "Walk on!"

The carriage lurched forward as Camden was led away.

"Matthew—the gentleman—even he seemed to believe that I am still in danger. I thought it was Camden, but now?" How could I know for sure?

Matthew positioned himself to see through the window. He provided no answer.

If not him, who? And why? A sob caught in my throat.

The road to Plymouth was long and tiresome. And yet, I felt pulled back to the only home I'd ever known. Was it because I was driven by fear? Or was I compelled by God to go there? I couldn't distinguish one feeling from the other. Regardless, I hoped He guided us. And believed that He did.

A half-hour later, and as the sun positioned to hide from sight, we arrived. The child had grown restless and spent some time standing and bouncing up and down while holding onto the carriage seat. Now, he was hungry and tired. I felt the same. The coach pulled to a stop and the coachman shouted to the stable boy. I prayed there would be room inside the inn.

We needed food and rest. But Matthew had loaded the gun and cocked the hammer, a finger lifted to his lips.

The babe whimpered. I expected someone to open the door and help me down. No one appeared.

Matthew flashed a look. "Get down on the floor, and hold the babe down, no matter if he screams. Do you understand?" I nodded.

Matthew lifted the latch of the door and paused, looking right and left. I hunkered low, the babe squirming and whimpering, protected beneath me.

"Sorry, sir. Lost my footing." The coachman appeared with a toothy smile, and Matthew visibly relaxed and lowered the weapon. "After riding with that gentleman, I don't wonder that you're a little skittish."

Matthew jumped down and the coachman handed me out of the coach, then I scooped up the baby.

"You ain't got nuthin' to worry about with me, young folk." He motioned to the inn, sweeping his hat from his head. "Take your repast. I thank ye sir, miss."

Matthew slowly eased the hammer down to keep the pistol from firing. We both took in the fresh air. Would I ever be able to breathe properly again?

He secured our room quickly and requested our supper to be brought up. We dashed up the stairs behind the maid who toted the milk and ale with hunks of dry bread. No matter, we were too hungry to care. As soon as the door opened and the tray set down, Matthew shooed the maid away and locked the door behind her.

"Eat—and you and the babe get some sleep. I will keep watch."

Exhaustion flooded every part of my being. "Are you not also tired?" I knew he was.

He ran a hand through his hair like Ewan did when he was tired. "I am, but I can't let anything happen to you. And won't."

I tried to find words to reassure him, but could not. He had once endured evil and lived to tell about it. What more could I say? My thoughts tripped over themselves, my feelings too low to articulate.

He nodded towards the bed. "Get some rest."

I fed, cleaned, and changed the babe, then ate my chunk of bread—drank the ale. Then nestled the boy beneath the blankets, close beside me. Tears wanted to come but would not. Ewan's dear face—his dear chipped tooth smile, so handsome. *God...God... hear my cry. Hear my cry...Please return him to me.*

My body gave me no choice but to sleep. Soon, I knew nothing but the soft sound of rain in the distance of my dreams.

I woke with a start at first light. Matthew sat peering through the window. I whispered to him, "Matthew. Your turn. Get some sleep."

He rubbed his eyes. "Alright. But only for an hour. Then wake me. Will you promise?"

"I will."

He slipped beside the babe and fell asleep before his head hit the pillow. I took his place at the window and leaned against the chilled pane. I wracked my brain for answers. I went over every detail. If Camden had only been trying to protect me, then...who from? And why? How had every detail become so tangled?

I thought back over the night and considered how Camden had come to my room, looking for me. How my gowns had been destroyed, how I'd been accosted in the stables that snowy afternoon. How my room had been ransacked, and my father's bible stolen. Then, my blankets and pillows were stabbed by whoever thought I rested beneath. Someone had chased Ewan and me down the road as we sought escape to Goodwyn Abbey. The same person who shot Dr. Rillian?

I tapped my fingers against my knee. And how did Camden hope to ensure my safety by kidnapping me? He seemed afraid for his own life. Very afraid. I was beginning to think he told the truth. He'd said he'd given up—that he was "so very tired..."

An hour later, Matthew sat up in bed, as if on cue. He cleared his throat and rubbed the light scruff on his jaw. "Mrs. Stevens. I've seen a man do things he wouldn't normally do—thinking he had no other options." He grimaced. "Betimes to save his own neck at the risk of others."

He picked up the flintlock, gazed down its barrel, then set it down. "I've also seen men destroy a life as though it were a gnat in the way. You might drive yourself mad trying to figure it out—I know that I did. But when it came down to it," he shrugged, "they wanted me out of the way. No real reason for what they did to me. I was simply in the way. A small insignificant disturbance in their machinations."

A small disturbance... I reached for the water pitcher, poured the freezing cold onto a towel, and patted my face. A small disturbance... a ripple in the pond. An unexpected return to Butterton, a shocking discovery about my great grandfather. What was it?

The small inheritance that had been tangled up in the courts—did it matter?

Matthew touched my shoulder. "I told you, you'll drive yourself mad if you try to figure it out." He peered from the window, left and right. "Looks clear."

The next coach would leave in a few hours. Would that we were in Chilham already. But I couldn't shake what Matthew had said. I truly wasn't connected to these situations. Yet, I'd showed up and stood in the way of something important to someone.

What was my small part in the larger picture?

Chapter Eighteen

I wish I could say that our journey to Chilham remained uneventful. But that would be untrue. A broken wheel, a twisted spring, heavy rains, and a crying babe made for a difficult journey. I longed for home and the comfortable embrace of my friends. A warm fire, a hot bowl of stew—oh and, of course, a pot of blessed tea. I would never take a simple, steaming cup of tea for granted ever again.

Matthew remained ever-vigilant. The closer we got to Chilham, the more we were able to breathe and to look about us in appreciation of the countryside, rather than looking for danger around every corner. Unfortunately, we eased our attention too soon.

We were but a few miles from home along an empty, rugged coastline when riders approached the carriage. We stopped. The two other women and the other child with us began to weep in fear.

I did not—how often had I wept along this journey? My tears had all dried. I only wanted Ewan to be safe – and us to be home. Wherever that was.

Matthew held a finger to his lips, quickly raised his loaded weapon, and cocked the hammer—as he had often done on our journey. I handed off the babe and unsheathed my dagger. Of an evening, Matthew had taught me a few things to protect myself. Would I be able to follow through should it come to that?

The coachmen shouted at the riders. "What do you? I've naught but women and children."

"Rich ones?"

"No."

"We shall see for ourselves."

It was true, I had no money. The pounds had whittled down to a shilling. The last of which went to purchasing our seats on the coach.

The door jerked open and Matthew offered a swift kick to the man's face. He stumbled back. The other highwayman leapt from his horse, weapon drawn. Matthew fired, blowing a flintlock from the highwayman's hand. He screamed.

In a flash, Matthew again kicked the other assailant in the face and flipped him on his stomach with his arms wrested behind his back. The other ran away, blood streaming down his arms.

The coachman was beside him in an instant. He cut a leather strap from his whip. "Here—tie him with this." He spat on the ground beside the man. "You'll be in the gaol, hung soon, no doubt."

The breath I'd been holding released. The women wept more quietly now. But I was stunned. What Matthew had done had been unlike anything I'd ever seen. A truly heroic action.

"Matthew." Twas all I could say.

"I told you." Sweat beaded down his forehead. "I won't let anything happen to you."

The coachman set a booted foot on the back of the highwayman, his pistol aimed at his head. "Take a minute, young sir. You have my sincere thanks."

Matthew strode several paces away, then back again. He opened his satchel and reloaded the flintlock.

"Mr. Carter's training?"

He nodded. Swallowed. His hand trembled.

"You did well."

He sniffed and wiped his face with his sleeve. "If I hadn't been assaulted and left for dead, then I would never be here—protecting you. Doing this."

There was a purpose in it. Certainly. I grabbed onto that. Onto Matthew's hope. Come what may, I would be stronger for it. If I chose to be like Matthew.

Needless to say, our arrival in Chilham caused no small stir at the gates of Glen Park.

"I am all astonishment! Abject astonishment!" Cried Sir Jones as we approached with nothing but the clothes on our backs and a babe in arms. He stood at the entry in his old green frock coat, a pipe clutched between his teeth—the dearest sight in all the world. "My dear, my dear...oh my dear. Get you into the house. At once."

We stepped over the threshold as Mrs. Jones gathered me and the wee one in her arms. The tears I thought had dried spilled out.

Matthew could be heard, appealing to Sir Jones in the foyer. Could the local magistrate be trusted?

"Indeed."

Yes, thank God. Yes. I knew the man.

Mrs. Jones called to Angel who had been lurking around the corner. "The babe needs a good supper and a good cleaning."

"Yes, mum."

"And send a pot of tea directly." She gently guided me to recline on the sofa. "Now, do tell me why you've returned in this bedraggled state—whatever has happened?"

I knew Mrs. Jones would be shocked if she could have read the first pages of my journal, had the pages survived. Indeed, her mouth hung open as I told the tale. Soon, Sir Jones and Matthew joined us.

Sir Jones rubbed his hands together. "I've sent for the magistrate, my dear." His brow wrinkled in concern. "To think you've suffered so! I cannot conceive it! And here we thought it a boon to send you to Butterton Hall!"

I lifted my hand with Ewan's ring. "I cannot regret that I went."

Mrs. Jones eyes grew bright, a smile tinged the corners of her mouth. "You've married? But who is he? Where is he?"

A fresh round of tears fell as Sir Jones poured the tea and handed cups around. At one of our stops, I'd sent a message to Goodwyn Abbey—to alert Lord Sherborne to our whereabouts. I prayed the message landed in the right hands. And that he looked for Ewan before coming here. He must.

We dined that night on hot potatoes, cold ham, and more tea. The simple meal tasted rich compared to the showy offerings at Butterton Hall, though far less costly in comparison.

Matthew behaved with the impeccable manners of a true gentleman, though I knew he hadn't a decent night's sleep since the night before my wedding.

I was bundled off to a warmed bed in the room I'd occupied last, while Matthew and Sir Jones spoke with the magistrate. Mrs. Jones tucked me in as she had when I was sick as a child. I didn't mind a bit when she patted my hand and prayed. "Rest, dear daughter. Joy will come in the morning."

My eyes were heavy after the meal and after the long ordeal. Ewan, Ewan...his name on my lips, his face the one of my dreams...

I woke several hours later but did not stir from the safety of my bed. I relished the comfort. Prayed and wept for Ewan, ever hopeful though wary. And thought back to how this monstrous tale had rattled into my life.

Ewan had no idea that sending for this poor relation would set in motion a shocking evil. He'd once said that the tail-end of society may move about unseen, as it were, with more velocity than the head gives it credit for. That we might do more as we pleased as the result of our position. And yet, how dependent we are upon those above us! Yet the heel may bruise the head, if I may be so bold as to borrow this promise.

I thought of Camden's weary household staff. How afraid they seemed. How dour the housekeeper had been—and unconcerned as to my comforts. I'd been a guest—and verbally considered part of the family—no matter the distance between Lady Camden and me.

Had my arrival been as though a small shove to a child's tower made of blocks? The final push that tipped the structure off balance?

A knock came to my door and Mrs. Jones rushed in. Her gray curls poked wildly free from her cap. "You won't believe who is here!"

"Jane!" A man shoved past her. Ewan. It was Ewan!

He gathered me in his arms and held me close. "Jane, Jane. I thought I'd lost you."

"I didn't know if you survived!" I clung to his neck, all shyness gone from my regard for him.

He pulled back, stroking my long, tangled hair away from my face. "I was terrified I'd never see you again."

"How did you know where I'd be?"

"When I discovered Matthew had also disappeared, I only hoped he had followed you and hadn't been captured as you'd been." Fear still tinged around his eyes.

"I am not harmed, Ewan." My eyes scoured his face looking for injuries.

"Thank God." He gathered my hand in his and pressed it against his heart. "I found out the road the carriage had taken—the stable boy had been sorely misused. Lied to. Camden claimed an emergency. You traveled all the way to Cornwall!"

"I didn't know how I was going to find out where he'd taken you. I prayed desperately. Strangely enough, I met an older gentleman just as soon as I made it into the village. In tow, was Camden himself. A runner held him fast."

"The gentleman from the carriage—he wouldn't tell us his name."

"No. He did not tell me of it either, though such a visage as he bears, he is a man hard to forget." Ewan stroked my arm. "He told me of a young man and woman with a baby—and where they traveled. I've been a day behind you the whole journey. Always looking, always hoping. No matter how I tried to catch up to you, you and Matthew were always a step ahead."

A mere day's distance? My heart burst at the thought of how close we'd been the whole time. My love had pursued me. Chased me. The petitions I'd prayed over and over again had already been answered, but I did not know it. He'd come for me. Had always been coming for me.

"Thank God, you are all safe." He stroked my hair, my cheeks. Pressed a kiss to my lips. "I rode all night when I realized you'd go to Chilham—to Sir Jones."

A tear slipped down his face. I brushed it away across the sandy scruff along his jaw. "You would be amazed at Matthew's skills as a defender."

"Would I?"

I told of being stopped by highwaymen and what he'd done.

"Dear God. What might have happened…" His eyes shuttered closed then opened again, the blue of them brighter than before. "You don't think they pursued you in particular?"

"No. I don't. Though after seeing Matthew in action, I will never second-guess his ability again, no matter his youth."

"The old man—he confided that you still may not be safe though he had Camden by the neck."

"Camden begged me to believe that he'd only been trying to keep *me* safe. To protect me." I held up my sore wrists, still healing. "But that doesn't make sense. Why would he hurt you and bind me?" His pleading eyes—his exhaustion had bade me to believe him.

Ewan sat back. "He knew I'd never let you out of my sight—or trust him. Not after what happened under his roof."

"You think he told the truth?"

"A partial truth only. Something holds him back. And I think that something—or someone—has a lot to do with the Banbury scandal. Necks are on the line and he's scared that he might be next. There are those whose involvement was easily discovered and those who have been able to keep their doings under wraps, so to speak. The law chases the offenders on one side, and someone else threatens them from the other. That someone has lost their senses. Utterly."

Tea had been brought, we held the hot, steaming cups between us. I savored the moment.

"You once asked if madness lived at Butterton Hall—when your clothing had been strangely destroyed. Remember? And Lady Camden's easy dismissal?"

"Was the first most terrifying experience I'd endured to date, other than being told a dagger had been plunged into my pillows."

He sipped his tea. "And how odd it was to see a woman of society sink into illness—declaring the Hogmanay curse had come upon the house..."

"Yes. The doctor had to come for a few days—and then—the household staff had grown fearful. Mary—she ran. To Goodwyn."

"Jane. I believe the answer lies at Butterton Hall."

The answer was my assailant. And that person was...no. I couldn't believe it possible. Lady Camden. She'd been playacting the whole time. I swallowed at the lump in my throat.

"Must we return?" I sensed the answer.

Ewan rubbed his unshaven jaw. "I want to take you as far from Butterton as possible, but first..."

The babe's distant mewing answered the question. He'd clung to me and probably missed the security of my presence. And, he needed to be returned to his rightful place. With Tobias at Mayfield Manor. I couldn't fathom how difficult the journey would be unless he was with someone familiar.

That would be me. I closed my eyes against it.

"The Chinworth child—I didn't believe Camden told the truth about knowing his location. I thought he was lying to get what he wanted."

The box of papers that proved what he wanted to hide...

"Camden took me right to him. Begged to care for him while he had another job for the nurse."

"Did he say what kind of job?"

"No." I didn't know if she returned with Camden to discover the child and I had gone.

"The child seemed cared for?"

I nodded. Unfortunately, I'd seen little ones who'd been neglected, beaten, and hungry. "The Chinworth babe is plump and hale." His cry echoed down the hall. "He has a healthy set of lungs too."

Our door flung open. Mrs. Jones returned. "My husband begs you to join him downstairs in the library. He has something to show you." She smiled. "Come, Mr. Stevens. She will be down presently."

Ewan kissed my hand and left me to dress. Thankfully, Mrs. Jones brought an old gown of mine I'd left behind and draped it across a chair. Felt good to dress in something familiar. I almost felt myself again—but nothing, no nothing would ever be the same.

Chapter Nineteen

"My dear." Sir Jones rubbed his hands together as he paced along the sparsely filled shelving of the once grand room. The carpet had grown so threadbare, they'd rolled it up—leaving the wood flooring to show worn paths along the shelf lines. *Much traveled in my youth.*

"I didn't think it important at the time, indeed, twas but a conundrum. I didn't tell you because," he opened his hands as though they might do the telling, "they were your father's private thoughts, written in his private journals. He'd given them to me, remember dear? As he lay dying."

"Yes. He wanted you to have them and bid me to accept his decision in the matter." *Though it stung a little at the time, I wanted to please my father. I'd allowed the three leather-bound volumes to be passed into Sir Jones' hands.*

Sir Jones bowed. "He said that if there were any testimony that might encourage my faith within, I might glean from them and trust God's faithfulness all the more."

Ewan's arm slid around my shoulder. *Did he sense how much I had loved my father?*

"I've been rereading them and came upon an unusual entry. Not until you arrived last night and told your story, did I understand." He picked up the journal, marked with a scrap of foolscap. "At least, I understand that there is more I do not understand."

"I'm confused." I laughed at the irony.

He looked at me over his spectacles. "It is indubitably important. Perhaps it can answer one of your questions that I do not know to ask myself, you see," he tapped his graying temple, "I simply cannot carry everything you recounted to me in this old head of mine."

"May we read what you found, sir?"

"Ah, yes. Here."

I took the offered volume and read:

August 22, 1809

The past cannot reclaim what has been utterly changed and redeemed. Neither mine, nor my grandfather's who evidently sought to turn his life into something it hadn't been before. That "something" he sought was never found. Were it not for my good mother, whose roots were indeed held fast in good soil, bearing fruit, and bringing me up to know its goodness, I know not how I might have been influenced by my own father's wandering ways.

A tempter has come to me.

Someone who makes claims about my grandfather—they appear to be true. I cannot deny the mystery surrounding the tall, formidable man I once knew, nor the strange objects found within his ownership. Objects no common folk might enjoy. They are long gone, but I remember them. That memory gives me pause. I received another letter today from the Chinworth man. He knows much. Much more than I expected. After sending his son away, I thought not to hear from him again. Their desire for secrecy makes my bones restless. Such secrets taint any motivation I might have had for pursuing knowledge of my grandfather's past.

I'd been told that we were but cousins—of a distant sort. Not well connected. This too, a fabrication? Do I indeed live a lie and beg my daughter to do the same? What does one do with the truth if that same truth rots from within? To be sure, there is the stink of death about it. Chinworth compels me to decide. I have decided. God has ordered my steps and set my path. I will instruct Chinworth to burn what remains of my connection to Butterton Hall. It is a life not meant to be lived or God would have shown me otherwise, I am certain.

The small inheritance soon going to court will, in all probability, remain floundering in the courts. I hope that my dearest daughter never pursues it. Better to leave it all behind. I feel such foreboding. I must pray.

The box of papers. Father had asked Chinworth to burn them. No wonder Tobias couldn't find them, they no longer existed.

"His journal entry is reminiscent of the letter Tobias found." Ewan rubbed my back. "I wish I could tell you that would be the end of the issue."

I knew what he meant to say. That my connection to Butterton, while evidence had been destroyed, I was still an heir. And that the attempts on my life proved it. The unwitting heiress was in someone's way, with or without said proof.

"May we take this journal? His words may be of some use."

Angel brought the babe to me, his little arms reaching for the only comfort he'd known since being snatched from his nurse. Poor thing. He snuggled close.

Ewan smiled. "You'll be a natural mother someday."

My cheeks warmed.

"Let us take this day to rest—then, we ought to be on our way. I'll send a message to Sherborne, posthaste." He wrapped his other arm around me. "This isn't quite the honeymoon that I intended for us."

"What? No wife-napping, baby-snatching intrigue?"

"Certainly not." He bent to kiss my lips. "I'd hoped for a much more enjoyable holiday."

Someone took the babe from my arms. Mrs. Jones?

His arms came about me, he held me closer than he ever had, trailing kisses down my cheek. What was he thinking? Sir Jones must be mortified by our behavior. I looked around Ewan. We were alone. Quite alone.

"Thank God, you are safe." He slid his hand through my hair, sending the pins from the chignon, and tendrils down my back. He cradled my head as he kissed me yet again. "The moment I saw you, I was struck. I knew—though I cannot explain it—that you were to be mine."

I pushed away. "You thought I was a maid."

"Well...there was that. But in truth, when we dined together your first night at Butterton," he kissed the side of my lips, "I felt it as though it were the truth. An unavoidable fact." He laughed softly. "I was quite restless about it, didn't sleep for a few nights."

"I'm not sure there's such a thing as being love-struck." I'd felt an immediate attraction to him too.

"Isn't there?" A glint sparked in his eyes. "I didn't think so either until I met you."

"I suppose God can strike a man's heart to love in an instant if He so—" His lips pressed down upon mine again, soft and tender. Loving.

Did God orchestrate my romance? My heart pounded at the sweetness of it. I was beginning to think He did. Of course He did. Isn't that what I always believed? I just didn't think it was true for me, somehow...

He leaned his forehead against mine. "You are so very beautiful."

Feet shuffled into the room. "Oh—ah. Not again." Matthew grumbled and backed out of the room. "I have to deal with Sherborne and Elaina being lovebirds..."

"Wait, Master Dawes." Ewan pulled away. "Come. I have heard tales of your bravery."

Matthew folded his arms. "I did my duty."

"More than duty for you, wasn't it?"

Matthew looked away but drew his eyes back again. "When this is over, I will continue to train with Mr. Carter. I know I have Banbury's estate to deal with soon, but I hope my life can count for more than the wealth that has come to me. To be perfectly honest? I don't want it. But God has seen fit to put it into my care. Sherborne says I can trust Him." He laughed nervously. "I suppose I'll have to."

I wonder, did Matthew Dawes inherit more than wealth from his wicked predecessor? Did he inherit Banbury's enemies? I shuddered to think. No wonder the boy had to learn how to defend himself.

Ewan and I spent the day on a long walk. The magistrate assured me that no strangers had entered the village other than the highwayman Matthew had taken in. A search had been made for his partner.

I wanted to show Ewan everything. The manse where I'd spent my childhood, the church. I led him to the altar where I'd dream of wedding my future husband.

Ewan took my hands and repeated his vows to me, and I to him. We visited my father's grave in the kirkyard, then along the village shops and kind neighbors I had known.

By the end of the day, Mrs. Jones had conjured a feast to celebrate our wedding and included some of my oldest friends. Twas a glorious evening, a point at which I could pause and be thankful, even for the hardship that had brought us here.

Amid the candle glow, much laughter and food were shared—and far too many tales of my childhood antics. I'd never seen Ewan laugh so freely. He told a few of his own stories about his youthful days—and of his young siblings.

I couldn't wait to live life with him. Like this. With joy blooming on every side.

A few gifts had been left behind to remember our day by. Lace that Mrs. Hurst made herself—a costly length that she, no doubt, had planned to sell to fill her dinner plate. A silver tea set from Sir Jones and his wife—said to have been my mother's once upon a time. And a strange silver candlestick fashioned round a leaping horse from Mr. Creighton—also said to have come from my family.

Later, Ewan studied it. "I've seen one like it before. Its match stands at Butterton Hall, on the mantelpiece in Camden's study."

"You are certain?"

His lips quirked as he eyed me seriously. "Yes. You do know that I didn't marry you to think I might gain Butterton?"

"We probably won't gain Butterton back." Not that I ever had it in the first place.

"Mm."

"Would you wish it?" I plied him.

"I rather like my average solicitor's life. I desire a cozy townhouse for us, and little to do with society if I can help it, beyond that of my daily duties. But I keep thinking about what Matthew said. He's accepted what's come to him." He looked around him. "Your Sir Jones and his wife, they are not par for the course, are they?"

"No. Not at all." They'd always been a ready help to anyone in need. What little that had been in the family coffers hadn't dwindled because of gambling and intrigues. Sir Jones believed in using up what he had. Wear a thing out, stretch it, bless with it, and beyond. They had no son to inherit Glen Park, nor grandchildren to provide for. A societal oddity, to be sure.

He toyed with my hair, winding an end around his finger in a long coil. "If you gain Butterton, I believe you've been given an excellent example of how to proceed."

"Ewan?"

"Yes?"

"I love you." I meant it with every fiber of my being.

He cupped my face in his hands. "It was your life being in danger that forced us to marry quickly."

"True."

"I would have wanted to marry you all the same."

And we know that all things work together for good to them that love God, to them who are called according to his purpose...

Father may not have wanted to go anywhere near the original family line—and I believe God truly did guide his steps to be here, in Chilham, serving the people. But that didn't mean that God hadn't sent me back—for what purpose beyond stretching my faith and giving me a husband, I didn't know. Not even my father's attempt at closure could prevent it...

Ewan pulled me closer to him as we reclined before a crackling fire in the library. I slipped my arm over his chest and nestled there. He was my true home. Forever, I hoped.

Chapter Twenty

The journey back to Butterton was much different than before. Instead of being accompanied by a cold and distant housekeeper, I traveled with my husband. And Matthew, and of course the babe.

We talked much, laughed much, told many stories. Soon, Matthew had opened up about his life before Dawes Shipping had been wrecked by Banbury's schemes.

As soon as we came onto Butterton's main roads, a man riding a horse came alongside. I tensed at the sight.

Matthew peered from the window. "It's but one of Sherborne's men. Probably sent to keep watch for us." He closed the curtain. "Not to fear, Mrs. Stevens."

We had a delivery to make to Mayfield Manor—to Tobias. Had Sherborne alerted him? Or had we arrived before my message?

As we drew in front of the estate, Tobias ran from the entry, a woman behind him—and the vicar.

"Tell me it's true? Do you have him?"

Ewan opened the carriage door and handed me out. I picked up the babe who'd become alert since stopping and whispered in his sweet, tiny ear. "You are home now." I turned, and gave him to his uncle.

Tobias received him into his arms. Tears coursed down his face. "I've lost so much." He told the child. "My brothers—your father, my father too. But here you are. Returned to me."

The babe laughed at him and poked his nose.

"Oh is that the way of it, lad?"

The woman giggled behind him.

"Come, Tessa. See how strong he is! I can see that he is a Chinworth. Through and through."

The woman named Tessa smiled at the babe. "He is handsome, like his uncle."

Tobias smiled down at her. Much like Ewan had smiled at me. A blush crept upon her cheeks.

Tobias took my hand with his free one and gave a gentle squeeze. "Mrs. Stevens. I heard from Sherborne that you endured a great deal. I cannot imagine. I thank you for returning him safely to us." He motioned to the open door. "Please, come inside. We think it best if you reside here for the time being. Sherborne will be along shortly."

I entered an elegant atmosphere, far grander than that of Butterton Hall, though not quite as old. We were ushered through the library and to an adjacent private room. A fire had been lit, and the remains of tea sat upon a tray.

Tobias smiled. "You may congratulate us. Tessa and I were married soon after you left." He took her hand. "I'll never deserve her."

She kissed his cheek. "It's never about deserving."

Sherborne strode through the room with Carter on his heels. "Camden's been busy, I hear." He nodded to me. "Glad to see you all in one piece." His attention flashed to Matthew. "A word." He waved him over to the library for a private talk.

Carter bowed and sat close. "Tell me, how did Matthew handle the worst of it? Did he get sick? Cry? Grow weak in the knees and collapse when the difficulty ended?"

"No. He trembled for a few minutes afterward, but no. He held himself well. You should be proud."

Carter dipped his head. "I am, but it's taken well over a year for him to be so strong in his mind." He glanced at him through the doorway, then back at me. "I wonder what affected the change?"

"Determination, probably. He wasn't trying to save himself this time, but me and the babe. I don't know what I would have done without him."

"Thank you." He stood. "I must see to my student." He strode into the library trading places with Sherborne who joined us.

"Right then. Let's hear everything. Start to finish, don't leave out a single detail."

After we'd repeated everything we knew, Sherborne tapped his fingers against his coffee cup. "You believe Lady Camden to be the one who has tried to murder you?"

I took a deep breath. "I hope I am wrong, but it adds up."

"I can see what you are saying. We must try her, do you understand? Catch her in the act."

Ewan jerked. "Jane must not come to any danger."

Sherborne held his hands out. "No, no. Of course not. But still. Tomorrow is a calling day." He smiled. "What if we, as a group, simply went calling. You may beg her congratulations on your wedding Mr. Stevens." He set his cup down. "We gentlemen may beg to visit Camden's stables, and give you a minute alone. Only we won't be in the stables…"

Ewan sat on the edge of his seat. "What do you propose?"

"Most of the staff have fled Butterton. We won't be noticed."

"You mean that Lady Camden may make an attempt, we will witness enough to stop her in time?"

"She's an old woman, I don't imagine she'll get very far."

Ewan stood. "I won't have it."

I stayed him with my hand. "One way or another, this needs to end. I cannot live my life knowing someone is out to end it." I gulped. "I want to do it."

"Well then." Lord Sherborne's assured smile bespoke strength. "By visiting hours tomorrow, she will know that you've returned." He stood to leave. "I shall alert the magistrate—see if he's free of an afternoon's frolic."

That night, I slept fitfully in the arms of my husband.

If Lady Camden were the culprit, we would soon know.

The next morning, everyone was quiet on the road towards Butterton Hall. When we arrived, Ewan pressed a kiss to my cheek with the quiet reassurance of his love.

To say that Lady Camden was shocked to see us was an understatement. We sat in her drawing room, her in the center as though upon a throne. She gave no indication that she knew what had come of her husband.

"He is away on business." Was all she said.

He was away—true. He'd been captured and kept for questioning by the law. No doubt found more safety behind bars than here. Did death hang like a threat over him too?

Lady Camden's turban was a shimmery golden hue today. "I should have liked to throw you an engagement ball, my dear. No need to have run from here as though fleeing to Gretna Green. No indeed!" Her jeweled fingers wagged at Ewan, "Consider yourself reprimanded, dear. Thoroughly reprimanded. Stealing my cousin away like that when you knew I wanted the privilege of marrying her off myself."

"Ma'am." He bowed.

"I am simply devastated that the fox hunt was so rudely interrupted."

The gentlemen glanced at one another.

Sherborne quipped. "Indeed. For one so esteemed as Chinworth to die just as the fun began— however, the party did make a great show of emotion when they heard of his death."

Murder...it wasn't merely a death, but murder.

"Emotion? For Chinworth?" Her knuckles whitened over the arms of her chair. "He was going to—he was—" her words tumbled over the other in a garble. Was that a tear in her eye? "Ruin us."

Sherborne approached her chair and gently lay a hand on her arm. "Because of his need to tell the truth concerning Banbury?"

Her chin quivered and she brought out a lacy handkerchief. "You don't know the half of it." She swiped at her eyes, patted around her nose. "I would speak with my cousin. Alone if you don't mind."

It was time. She would make her move, if one were to be made.

Ewan and Sherborne rose from their chairs. Ewan bowed, his expression unreadable. "We shall pay a visit to the stables. I am rather fond of Camden's band."

The men left me alone. I knew that Carter had already slipped into place. Matthew too. I wasn't truly alone with her, come what may. My heart knocked against my chest as she patted the chair beside hers. I approached on weak legs—how I wished I might overcome this sense of fear!

"My long-lost cousin." She smiled. "You know, I couldn't wait to meet you again. When we stayed in your parent's home those many years ago, I envied what your mother had. A cozy manse, a child, a husband that adored her." She sniffed and dabbed the handkerchief once again. "Our children didn't survive."

"I am sorry." I swallowed a dry throat.

She waved her hand as she did that day when I told of my destroyed gowns. One couldn't dust away a tragedy with the swish of a hand.

"I saw something in your parent's home. Something that I was too familiar with. It was in your house."

Did she speak of the candlestick—of a like I'd only spied here at Butterton Hall?

She inclined her head as though looking into the past. "I shouldn't have been surprised, really. But how could I know just how closely we were truly related?" She reached for my hand and held it tightly. "I'd been lied to, so I discovered years later. It was all very confusing, I must say. Knotted family lines. Missing pieces turning up in strange places."

She looked into my eyes as if hoping to find the truth of what I knew there. She was more perceptive than I realized.

"Ah. I see." She gripped my hand tighter. "My father was a stern man." She let the fact hang as though I might understand this kind of father. I'd seen them yes. But not experienced one. "I have other nieces, you see, who have no knowledge of this. They are completely unaware that there is a woman before them who is due what rightfully belongs to her."

"But the death certificate..."

"Posh. I have proof. Much proof." She moved her hand from mine and pulled a ring from her finger. She held it out to me. A small sapphire rested among a vine of silver leaves. "This belonged to your great-grandmother upon her wedding. You shall have it. And more besides."

Perhaps I knew what she did not: the Camden coffers were depleted. Empty.

I took the ring. "Lady Camden, I am not here to require Butterton Hall from you."

"No?"

How much should I tell her? Did she know how often my life had been at risk during my stay? I'd thought the evidence pointed towards her—but now I wasn't so sure. She was all but handing me the keys to Butterton. I, her greatest competition...

I thought back to Lord Camden's plea—that he'd only tried to protect me. From whom?

"Lady Camden, who is trying to kill me?"

Her lips parted and she clasped a hand over her mouth. "No—no, dear. It isn't so! The Hogmanay curse has lifted—the vicar prayed! After your accident, he prayed!"

It wasn't theatrics then—her belief in the curse.

The housekeeper carried in a pot of tea. So—the woman had recovered. She handed Lady Camden a cup, then one to me.

Matthew stood in the doorway, making hand signs to stop me as Carter slipped from behind the drapery.

Lady Camden and the housekeeper both startled at their sudden appearance.

Matthew shouted. "Don't drink it, Mrs. Stevens. She put something in your cup!"

Rothy threw the steaming pot at Matthew, who dodged it as it crashed to the floor, shattering into a thousand pieces.

"Get a hold of yourself, Rothy." Lady Camden stood. "What is the meaning of this?"

The housekeeper pulled a kitchen knife from beneath her apron and reached for me. I threw myself across the room, just as Carter and Matthew took her down.

Ewan and Sherborne ran in, Ewan gathered me by his side and held me tight.

"You!" The housekeeper spat at me. "I tried to scare you off, but you wouldn't go."

It was she. The housekeeper. It made no sense..."So you tried to kill me instead?"

"That stupid maid saw me."

Mary...had her life been threatened?

Her lips sneered, even as they trembled. "Better you die by my hand than another's."

"Another's?"

"My son. Butterton Hall rightfully belongs to *my son*."

I didn't know she had a son.

Shame swept Lady Camden's face. "Our gamekeeper. My father had...an indiscretion before marrying my mother."

"Indiscretion, you call it? He *married her*!"

Lady Camden swayed on her feet and sat down. "There was never proof."

"I have a marriage certificate." She struggled against Carter's hold.

"It is a false one, and well you know it."

Lord Sherborne approached. "Regardless of your claims, I'm rather struck by the fact that you tried to end the life of this innocent woman."

"She was going to take what was rightfully mine. If I didn't do it, my son was going to." Tears coursed down her wrinkled cheeks. "I couldn't let him have that on his conscience. Not that too."

Sherborne's brow lifted. "Too?"

"My granddaughter married Samuel Chinworth—and where did that get her? Dead. Someone had to pay."

My voice trembled, "Your son murdered Mr. Chinworth?" Because Tobias' brother had died, retribution had to be paid upon his father?

She didn't deny it. Must be true.

"*Rothy...*" Lady Camden shook with rage.

The housekeeper continued. "That horrid man called Brown kept coming around. He was helping Chinworth." Once again, she strained against Carter's hold.

"How do you know this?" Ewan asked.

"Because Chinworth took what was coming to us—to Camden and me. I overheard Camden's plans for gain, I did. I told him so. Threatened if he didn't share." She laughed a pitiful laugh. "Threatened to expose the truth about my mother's marriage. Among other things. Seems the name of Banbury is sufficient to strike fear in many a man these days. Didn't know your husband was afraid of me, did you *Lady Camden*? My son found him—the one helping Chinworth—wandering about on New Years Eve. Did him in. Once and for all."

Except he hadn't died right away. He'd stumbled into Butterton Hall—and onto our New Year's party. *None shall have it! No Banbury gets the last word. Not when I gone through the trouble. A curse, it is. A curse.* Whatever he'd buried, he had done so before the gamekeeper—the housekeeper's son—killed him.

Chinworth had been next. Then, her sites had fixed upon me. What Chinworth had tried to interrupt and righten had been stopped. Yet Ewan had found proof that would create another unanticipated problem. A ripple in the plans to fill Butterton's coffers. But the housekeeper had already known. As had Lady Camden.

Carter nodded to Sherborne who exited the room.

I licked my lips and added my quick equations. "So, you and Camden were after the same thing—and thought that by bartering the Chinworth babe—your grandchild, no less, that you would gain...?"

Rothy sneered. "What Camden promised me."

Ewan stepped closer to her. "What exactly did he promise you?"

"Gold."

Gold. Is that what the man had buried before her son killed him? Must be. The man was right. It was a curse. The desire for gold over the life of a human.

"In exchange for your silence?"

"He was to give me every document pertaining to Butterton's ownership. I would keep silent as long as I was paid." She squirmed on the floor like an animal. "We held each other's secrets, he and I."

I blinked as though waking. This woman had accompanied me from Chilham all the way here. She might have ended my life at any point. Why hadn't she? I recalled how tired she'd been upon arrival. How we lurched along the same long road to

Butterton. How her hands were still, though it appeared she'd been knitting.

The sock.

There'd been a baby's sock left on the seat.

"You stole away your grandson." And Camden had helped her.

She shrugged. "There's more than one way to skin a cat."

She'd meant to blackmail Tobias with his nephew. For herself—and her son. Did she consider the babe at all?

"Then you had to go and marry that snooping *solicitor*! His sense of duty ruined everything. I knew what he'd found—and how he'd been digging around the registers at the church." Her body relaxed and she drew her knees to her chest. "When my son couldn't find you the night you'd flown..."

The shot in the wood—and later, Dr. Rillian had been wounded... An easy mistake for a gamekeeper to think he shot upon poachers. Only it had been me he'd hunted. To think, we were blood related by some fraction, only he didn't care. His grudge against the heritage of his past enabled the curse of Cain.

"Camden saw me enter your room. Knew what I'd tried to do. He tried to poison me, but I was too strong to die."

Camden had fled, Dr. Rillian said. He'd fled to find me. And rescue me?

"I sent my son to follow you and finish the job once and for all."

Only Camden had kidnapped me first. He'd been telling the truth. Why had he bound and gagged me? Perhaps he knew that I wouldn't believe him. That I was already afraid of him and would do everything to get away. If he'd unbound me too soon, then I might have—I shuddered to think of the gamekeeper on my heels—a man I'd only seen but once, the day of the fox hunt. He might have ended my life, regardless of Ewan's protection. And Camden knew it.

So he took me to the Chinworth babe. Had he been attempting to right the wrongs as Chinworth had tried to do?

The magistrate strode in, Sherborne just behind him.

Carter lifted Rothy to her feet. "Take her."

"Take me, you won't get much now. I'm to die soon."

The magistrate and another man removed her from Butterton, loaded her into a waiting wagon, and sped away.

Lady Sherborne clutched her chest as tears streamed down her face. "I can't bear to be living in this curse!" She leaned bent over into her lap. "You know where my husband is, don't you?

Simpson strode into the room and bowed. "I thought I heard a commotion. Might I be of service, ma'am? A cup of chocolate, perhaps?"

Chapter Twenty-One

"We are ruined, Jane. Ruined."

"We still live and have breath, Lady Camden. There is much to live for." I glanced at Ewan.

"I'll not have you inherit a curse."

"I cannot inherit a curse. I depend upon the promises of God, as you must also."

She sniffed through more tears. "Send for the vicar, Simpson. Don't dwaddle."

"I am here." The vicar's large, imposing frame filled the doorway. He offered a gentle smile to the humiliated woman. How had he known to come?

Ewan pulled me from the room as the vicar's comforting words of prayer began to flow from his lips.

"I forgot what a fine horse Camden had gifted to you. Let us go see how she fares."

A moment alone with my husband after that shocking experience was much needed. I stroked the beast's jaw, doing my best to breathe normally.

"It's a lot to take in." Ewan pressed a kiss to my cheek and rested his head atop mine.

"This is where I was attacked. By that woman." The housekeeper. I'd been nothing to her before my arrival. Nothing but a name on a distant family tree.

Like Matthew had said—I was but a small disturbance in her scheme. A ripple that would grow if more people found out about my great-grandfather. It was never really about me—not my soul—nor my character. Twas only about gain.

I continued to stroke the horse's jaw—and down her long, warm neck. A small mew met my ears and a creature rubbed against my leg. The cat. He blinked his eyes at me and mewed again.

"Ah, it is your little friend. She wouldn't leave your side that day..." Ewan bent to pet her. "What's this?"

He lifted the cat from the flagstone and traced the edges with his fingers. "Hand me that tool, Jane." He grasped the lever and lifted the stone from its place. There beneath it was a box.

"Ewan. Chinworth didn't burn the documents as my father requested after—" I stopped as he lifted the lid away. No, it wasn't the documents. It was the gold.

The gold the dead man had hidden. He'd called it a curse. The man had died trying to simply bury the evil of the Banbury scandal. *No one shall have it!*

One couldn't hope to merely bury a problem, no matter how great or small, and expect it to be utterly gone. No, it must come to the light of day to be dealt with.

I stared at the substance that too many had already suffered or died for. "What shall we do with it, Ewan?"

He released a breath. "Sherborne will know." He replaced the flagstone and pulled me into my arms. "You will always be my greatest treasure." He looked down into my eyes. "How do you fancy another journey in the carriage?"

"Banish the thought."

"I rather hoped we could finally enjoy a honeymoon."

He kissed me full and well until a groan met my ears.

"Not again!" Matthew.

Ewan laughed. "You just wait, Master Dawes. Your turn will come. And there will be no defense against the workings of the heart."

Epilogue

Many months later, whilst settling in our townhouse in London, I found a twenty-pound note tucked within my reticule.

"Ewan? What's this?"

"Buy nothing on credit, dear."

"I don't need to carry such an amount—" And then, I remembered. A twenty-pound note had been gifted me when I'd arrived at Butterton—and had helped Matthew, the babe, and I reach Chilham. Without it, we would have suffered. I'd assumed the gift from Lord Camden. But no. I looked at my handsome husband who was leaning over his account books, inking in numbers and notes.

"You gave it to me."

"Of course, dear."

"No, the first time. At Butterton."

He blushed and smiled. "Found me out, did you?"

His generosity had no doubt saved us. Before he knew me or loved me, his first action had been kindness.

I closed the drawstrings to my purse, set it aside, and crawled rather unceremoniously into his lap. He set his quill down and wrapped his arms around me. It would be several more months before we knew the fate of Lord Camden or Butteron Hall. Whatever the future held, I knew I could rest easy with such a man beside me.

Ann Elizabeth Fryer loves nothing more than using story and romance to relay the depths and graciousness of a Father who holds us securely in the palms of His hands. Ann, her husband, and three children make their home in small-town Illinois where they can hear church bells keep time and tradition.

Visit her website at annelizabethfryer.com

I am so thankful that God put fellow author Danielle Grandinetti in my life! What would I do without her continued support, cheerleading, keen eyes, and compassion? She is a daily gift.

I also want to thank Tamsey Bremer for her steadfast assistance proofreading the final copies when my eyeballs simply couldn't go another round. Colleen Rieke, my Mumsie, Kelly Hall, Annie Sotski, Asha Neal, my Mother-in-law—you girls know how to make this author feel good. God bless you!

And as always, John Perrodin, whose mentorship over the years has been golden.

Of Needles and Haystacks
    Of Horse and Rider
    Of Hearts and Home
    Of Time and Circumstance
    Of Pens and Ploughshares
    Butterton Brides Series:
    A Convenient Sacrifice
    A Favorable Match
    An Opportune Proposal

Printed in Dunstable, United Kingdom